Keeper of the Hourglass

The Life and Death of

Peter Nichols

G.L. Garrett

Black Rose Writing | Texas

ISBN: 978-1-68433-390-5
PUBLISHED BY BLACK ROSE WRITING
www.blackrosewriting.com

Printed in the United States of America
Suggested Retail Price (SRP) $17.95

Keeper of the Hourglass: The Life and Death of Peter Nichols is printed in Book Antiqua

*The final word count for this book may not match your standard expectation versus the final page count. In an effort to reduce paper usage and energy costs, Black Rose Writing, as a planet-friendly publisher, does its best to eliminate unnecessary waste without lessening your reading experience.

For Millie and Bradley

Keeper of the Hourglass

The Life and Death of

Peter Nichols

CHAPTER 1
An Unusual Awakening

It's as simple as this: we do not choose death; death chooses us. That's it…in the great rule book of life, there is just one page, and written on that solitary page is one and only one rule: death chooses us. Your status in life is of no consequence because death does not discriminate. White, black, tall, short, stocky, petite, old, young, none of this matters. So, when death came and took young Peter Nichols away, it should not have seemed unusual or tragic. It was just the way it was supposed to be, exactly as it was supposed to happen. Since the dawn of time, that was how things worked, and it would remain that way until Peter Nichols became the boy who changed it all.

Up until this point, Peter was as normal as any other kid his age. That is, outside of the fact he was awkwardly quiet and painfully shy. Those personality traits ended up causing Peter to be the target of a particular bully, Bobby, who as it so happened, also caused Peter to race into the road and be struck by a truck. Which finally brought us to where we are now.

It is when Peter slowly awoke, where he found himself lying on a hard, wooden bench – his eyes barely able to focus on his surroundings – and feeling extremely strange. It was a feeling as if he had held his breath for too long, and everything was tingling as though a thousand needles were pricking his skin. Even his hair was tingling. Trying to clear his vision, he blinked several times and squeezed his eyes shut tight.

"Ugh, I feel awful," he moaned, looking up expecting to see a bunch of people crowding around him, or worse, Bobby standing over him and laughing.

Instead, he sat up and realized he was alone in a large, unfamiliar room. Peter strained his eyes to focus, and as his vision returned, he saw that the room was huge. Not only that, the room was ornately decorated in darkly-stained wood-paneled walls stretched out to meet coffered ceilings with various crystal chandeliers suspended from long chains. Oil paintings, like the ones he remembered from museums, lined the walls.

Peter inhaled a faint but familiar odor that smelled like his grandfather's pipe. It had a sweet smell of cherries. He rubbed the back of his head and looked around, trying to figure out exactly where he was.

The room was unusually accessorized with hundreds of clocks and hourglasses of all shapes and sizes. Everywhere he looked, there were different types of clocks ticking, bonging, and chiming, all in unison. Each windowsill, table, shelf, and fireplace mantle was covered with hourglasses. Standing up, Peter noticed a large wooden table nearby with some pamphlets displayed on it. Perhaps those held some answers. He could then figure out where the heck he was, find a phone and call his parents to come and get him.

Before he reached the table, a sharp, nasally voice echoed across the marble and stone encased hallways, which ran off in every direction.

"You are supposed to report to room 2417!" the voice shouted.

This has to be the strangest hospital I've ever been in, Peter thought as he looked around to see where the voice had come from.

"Oh, I'm sorry," said the stranger's voice after Peter didn't respond. "Am I disturbing you?"

He still couldn't see who was addressing him and found himself turning in circles until a large podium caught his attention. It was so tall he couldn't see over the top.

"Perhaps we should all wait until you decide to finish your tour," the voice echoed.

"I'm sorry, I don't–" Peter tried to explain before the voice cut him off.

"Room 2-4-1-7! Down the hall then left, right, left, and you report to the room that is the twenty-seventh door on the left!"

More confused than he'd been five minutes prior, he just stood there until a little old man popped his head up from behind the podium.

"Oh, hey, um hi, I'm Peter," he said as he took off his baseball cap and smiled up at the little man who was leaning over the podium.

"Hmph," was the only response he gave as he looked Peter up and down.

The odd man was dressed in a starched, long-sleeved white shirt with a tall, stiff collar. One of the sleeves had a black armband around it, and he wore a gray tweed vest over his shirt. A gold pocket watch reflected a glimmering ray of light into Peter's eyes, causing him to squint. The little stranger also wore a green visor on top of his head, which dipped or cocked at certain angles depending on his mood. When Peter first saw him, his visor was bent upwards. At present, the visor was bent down the middle, making the old man appear quite angry, and he was now leaning even further over the large mahogany podium to get a better look at Peter, who held back his laughter at the interesting picture the man made.

"Well?" snarled the little man.

Peter didn't know what to say. He was mesmerized by the sight of this person who was bald except for a streak of bushy white hair above his ears. His sideburns, which were just as shaggy and just as white, ran down his face and met at what turned out to be an extremely large, even wilder, unkempt moustache. It was so bushy, Peter couldn't even tell if he had lips. The words just flowed through his moustache, which rustled with each breath. His forehead was crinkled, and he stared at Peter through squinty eyes set deep behind a pair of thick, round glasses, over which draped even larger and bushier white eyebrows.

"Is it that you do not understand English, or perhaps I am speaking with a mouthful of my lunch?" he asked as he looked at his gold pocket watch. "No wait, it is two hours and twenty-three minutes past the lunch hour, so that could not be it. As I stated so clearly to you not three point seven seconds ago, room 2-4-1-7, down the hall then left, right, left and it is the twenty-seventh door on the left. That is where you should have been thirteen minutes and forty-two, no wait, forty-three seconds ago!"

The strange little man shook his head, tucked the watch back into his pocket, and returned to what he had been doing behind the podium.

All Peter could do was stand and watch as the stranger shuffled some books around and scribbled on a stack of papers. Everything was so confusing, and Peter had a thousand questions running through his head – all of which made him forget where the little man told him he needed to go, but there was no way Peter was about to ask for a map or for him to repeat himself. So, instead, he walked over to a set of three identical hallways, each of which branched off of the large room, and each of which were seemingly endless. As he stood there staring, Peter hoped he could remember the directions he'd been given, but what was the point if he couldn't even tell which hallway to take?

"They're all the same," Peter muttered. "How am I supposed to tell one from another?"

Each of the hallways had a bright red carpet runner disappearing into an abyss of shadows. Polished brass chandeliers adorned the ceilings of the hallways, faintly illuminating the endless progression of brown wooden doors lining both sides. As Peter stood there, he became more and more nervous, and when Peter was nervous, he would fidget. He just stood there, shifting his baseball cap back-and-forth between his fingers. Several minutes had passed before he decided there was no other choice but to ask for the directions again.

"Ahem…" Peter nervously cleared his throat as he tried to gather up enough courage to interrupt the stranger.

The little man heard this, and let out an exasperated gasp. Not bothering to look up from his paperwork, he extended his thin, boney index finger to point down the first hall.

"Oh, right. Well, thank you," Peter said as he bowed for some reason before he walked toward the hall.

He couldn't help but stare at the man as he continued to work, stamping papers and books before transferring them from one pile to another. Fixated, Peter bumped into a door as he entered the hallway, making it slam against the wall. This prompted a not-so-pleasant look from his unknown greeter who just grunted and shook his head.

Peter continued down the hallway, making his first left as instructed. This hallway seemed to be an exact replica of the one he'd just turned from. It was long, wide, and had an untold number of paintings of an unknown number of old people on the walls. Peter bit his lower lip as he looked from door to door, trying to get an idea of whether he was in a doctor's office, a hospital, or anything similar. All the uncertainty made him anxious as his pulse raced. According to that stranger, Peter was late for something, but he wasn't sure what that something was.

Continuing down the hall, he kept looking for something that might tell him where he was, or more importantly, where he needed to be. There were no doctors, nurses, or patients to help him out, and he was now wondering if anybody had bothered to call his parents. As far as Peter knew, nobody knew his name. So how would they even know whom to contact?

"Maybe I should count the doors. One, two, three, no wait, the twenty-seventh door is not until the third hallway, which is up on my left, or is it my right?"

It felt like hours passed as Peter continued his journey through the hallways, each one an exact replica of the other. Once he got to the hallway he believed contained the room he was supposed to be in, Peter counted twenty-seven doors and looked up. A set of numbers affixed to a door identified it as room 2417.

"Finally!" He breathed a sigh of relief.

There didn't seem to be anything special about this door; it was tall and wooden, just like every other door he'd passed. No sign stated what the room was used for, or what was inside. He took a huge gulp of air, turned the large, round doorknob, and pushed the heavy door open. A slow creaking noise from the rusted hinges announced Peter's arrival. He cautiously entered the wood-paneled room, which contained two long wooden tables that ran along both sides. Behind the tables sat a number of people scribbling on pieces of paper in front of them. Peter immediately noticed he was by far the youngest person in the group, and when he closed the door, he felt as though everybody's eyes were on him.

"He's so young," one elderly woman whispered.

This room is bigger than my house, Peter thought, not really paying attention to what the woman had just said.

A large lump entangled itself in his throat as he nervously smiled and stood there looking around, trying to figure out what he was supposed to do. Finally, a woman's voice broke the silence and echoed a greeting to him.

"Welcome, Peter! Please come forward," she said with a warm smile.

He walked past the tables, the stares following him, making him more nervous than curious. Peter walked up to a large desk in the back of the room. A rather plump woman sat there smiling at him. She wore a pair of gold-rimmed glasses attached to a beaded chain that dangled from her neck, and a framed ivory cameo was attached to the collar of her white ruffled blouse. She reminded Peter of a librarian he had once seen.

"Well, I'm glad you finally found us," she said.

"I'm sorry I'm late. The man in the front–"

"Ahh yes. Mr. Grumsby. Not much of a socializer, but a very dedicated, knowledgeable man nonetheless. Here is your welcome packet and a quill," she said as she handed Peter a large folder with a feather lying on top of it.

He picked the feather up and looked at it, and then at her.

"Um, what am I supposed to do with this?"

"Oh, I'm sorry. Where is my head today?" she asked. "Perhaps a pen would suit you better."

The feather in his hand turned into a pen. Peter stared at it for a moment confused, but then brushed it off as another confusing part of a confusing day. He took a look at the packet, which was a large leather-bound folder but had no writing on the cover that could give Peter a clue as to what was going on.

"Please find a chair and complete the information inside," she told him. "If you have any questions Peter, my name is Hildegard Penntiworth, and I will be your counselor."

"Um, okay, thank you, Hil – I mean Miss Pentigard, WORTH! Miss Penntiworth," he nervously answered.

Miss Penntiworth smiled at Peter, put her head down, and returned to her writing as he turned around and walked toward an empty chair in the corner of the room. As he passed by each person, they would stop writing, look up, and give Peter an awkward smile before returning to their papers. Something didn't seem right, but nonetheless, Peter took a seat, opened his packet of information, and began to spread out all the documents. Stopping for a moment, he watched everybody else in the room. They all had their heads down and were scribbling away. Apparently, they knew what was going on.

I've never had to fill out insurance papers before, Peter thought. *This doesn't seem right.*

Tapping his pen against his head, Peter looked around before slapping the pen onto the table. He pushed back his chair with a squeak as it scraped across the floor. Some of the people looked up but then went back to filling in their forms.

"Sorry," Peter whispered as he got up from his chair and walked up to Miss Penntiworth.

"Um, excuse me, ma'am," he whispered.

"Yes Peter?" she said, looking at him over the top of her glasses.

He paused for a moment, now realizing he'd never told her his name.

"How did you…never mind," he said dismissively. "I'm sorry, Miss Penntiworth, but could you perhaps tell me where I am?"

Miss Penntiworth smiled, leaned across the desk until she was within a few inches from his face, then she adjusted her glasses to the farthest point of her nose, stared at him, and whispered in a calm, hushed voice, "Why Heaven of course."

The second she spoke these words, Peter froze, and as he stared into her eyes, the walls in the room crumbled around him and collapsed like shattering glass as though he was being swept into a dream. Clouds swirled and cascaded from Miss Penntiworth's eyes and filled the room until Peter was surrounded by empty sky. Frantic, he tried to grab something to hold on to as a scene familiar to him formed below his feet. He watched himself swing at the last pitch of the baseball game and strikeout. He winced as he saw Bobby Crones push him down into a wad of soft, wet bubble-gum in the dugout. A short time later, Peter saw the shadowed memory of his former self run out of the dugout in tears, jumping onto his bicycle and pedaled away as fast as he could down the road, with Bobby close behind.

Peter's attention turned back to his surroundings as the clouds around him grew darker, the wind picked up, and the air became cold. Peter looked below again just in time to see Bobby hurling rocks at him as he tried to escape, wiping the tears away, his heart racing. He then screamed when looking ahead, he saw the big delivery truck turning the corner. There was nothing he could do as the truck headed straight for him.

Helpless, Peter dropped to his knees, begging for his former self to stop before it was made all too clear what had happened. Frozen, he watched himself being thrown from his bicycle by the force of the truck, and as Peter collapsed back to the ground from the accident, he too collapsed, the truth of his situation overwhelming him. As it happened on the pavement of the road before, Peter's head now bounced off of the marble floor, and he lay there unconscious.

"Good Heavens!" Miss Penntiworth exclaimed.

She rushed from behind her desk and gently leaned him up against her.

"Peter…Peter…Wake up!" she said as she pulled a white lace handkerchief from her sleeve and waved it frantically in front of him.

Peter carefully opened his eyes and saw that everybody in the room was standing up out of their chairs and staring at him. At first, he looked at Miss Penntiworth, but quickly turned away, afraid of what he might see this time. The only thing he could think of at this moment was how to escape, so he started to wiggle away from her as fast as he could. When he finally pulled himself free, he crawled across the floor, with Miss Penntiworth trying to follow. When he reached the corner of the room, he curled up into a ball as Miss Penntiworth tried to calm him down.

"Peter, it's all right," she said to him slowly.

His breathing was fast, and he felt his heart thundering in his chest. Peter was rocking as he hugged his knees into his chest.

"What do you mean it's all right? Heaven? I can't be–" Peter couldn't bring himself to say the word. "I've got a math test I need to study for!" he said quickly.

Miss Penntiworth kneeled next to him for several moments, waiting until he caught his breath. As he started to breathe normally again, he couldn't help but open his eyes and glance at the other people in the room. Certainly, all of these people could not be dead. Some of them were his parent's age.

"Peter, please calm down. Let's take a walk," she said softly.

But it was no use. He just continued to hug his legs into his chest; his eyes were wide open, and he was trembling. Miss Penntiworth stood up and adjusted her dress, rubbing her hands across the ruffled material, smoothing it out.

"It's all right everyone," she told the other people in the room. "Please return to your chairs and complete your paperwork for me."

As they made their way back to their seats, Miss Penntiworth held her hand out to Peter.

She's got to be kidding, he thought.

This must have been a cruel joke somebody was playing on him. That was the only explanation. Somebody needed to explain to him what was going on and tell him who decided to pull this rotten prank.

But what if this wasn't a joke? He certainly remembered the accident, and what if…? He had to find out one way or another what was going on, so he slowly reached out for her hand. Of course, he wasn't sure what to expect when he grabbed it. Was this woman a ghost? And if she were, would his hand grab mist when he went to touch her? Was she going to feel cold and lifeless like that fish he found floating in Cooper's pond? But then again, she wasn't floating; she walked on the ground just like he did. His mind was racing.

"Peter, come with me, and I will explain everything," she said, coaxing him along.

She was his only hope; he had to figure all of this out. As he looked around, and then at her, he knew he had to listen to what she had to say. Miss Penntiworth took his hand and helped him to his feet. Surprisingly, her hand felt warm, soft, and comforting, just like when he used to walk hand-in-hand with his grandmother before he got too old for such things. Today, he welcomed that feeling again, wishing he could hold her hand once again, and never let go.

"Let's get some fresh air if you feel up to it, son."

They walked out of the room, down the hall, and entered a courtyard where they strolled along a winding cobblestone path. The green moss creeping onto the top of the stones cushioned Peter's feet. Large, lush trees lined both sides of the courtyard and flowers covered most of the ground, brilliantly highlighting every color of the rainbow.

Everything feels too real, Peter thought as he looked around. *Miss Penntiworth, the moss, the flowers, there's no way I'm dead.*

Everything he thought he knew about death was that it was cold and lifeless, but the moss he was standing on was green and soft and very much alive. The flowers filled the yard with a wonderful fragrance. This had to be a horrific joke.

"Who put you up to this?" he asked Miss Penntiworth sternly.

"Nobody put me up to anything, Peter. You have to believe me, and you have to believe yourself."

"No, this isn't right, and it isn't funny!" he urged. "Did Bobby make you do this?" He scrambled from tree to tree, looking for Bobby or any of his cronies that might be hiding and having themselves a good laugh.

But the longer he looked, the more worried he became that he wouldn't find the culprits. Peter had covered every inch of the courtyard, and much to his disappointment, it was only him and Miss Penntiworth left looking at each other. As he stared at her, he recognized the look of concern in her face.

"I'm sorry about this, Peter. I thought you knew."

Peter didn't know what to say. He stood there, staring at the ground, mumbling that he couldn't be dead. He then looked up at her, and a tear slowly rolled down his cheek.

"I'm just a kid," he whispered to her. "Why did this happen to me?"

"It happens to everybody, dear," she explained carefully. "Sooner or later everybody and everything passes."

"But I'm a kid. I haven't even kissed a girl yet, or driven a car."

Peter clenched his fists and grunted as he frantically began pacing back and forth. "Anyways, I can feel my heart beating. All I did was pass out. There's no way I can be dead."

Miss Penntiworth rested her hands in front of her. He looked back at her then to the ground. Everything was too strange. Nothing was making sense.

"Could this be true?" he whispered as he looked up to the sky. "Am I actually…"

His eyes drifted back to the ground.

"What did I do to deserve this?" he asked, hoping for some sort of answer from this woman, searching for something, anything that made sense.

"Peter, you didn't do anything. You are not being punished," she told him. "This is just the way your life was meant to turn out. There is nothing you could have done to prevent or to change this."

Hoping to focus on something else, he continued to stare at the ground, hoping to block out her voice, but his brain continued to spin.

"How can I help you dear? Let's discuss this."

Miss Penntiworth tried to get Peter to talk, but with a million thoughts running through his head, he couldn't focus long enough to form a sentence, let alone come up with any questions for her. He just walked along the stone path with his mouth half open. Miss Penntiworth caught up and put her arm around him, guiding him towards the building.

"Come this way, Peter. Maybe this will help. If nothing else, it might answer a few questions for you."

She opened a door and entered the building with Peter following close behind. They walked along several hallways and came to a common area where people were gathered drinking tea, laughing and joking with each other.

"Peter, this stage of death is quite like life. You feel no different than you did back home. You have your emotions, your feelings, and everything you would have otherwise. You will laugh and cry. Your heart will even skip a beat when you take a bite of a huge ice cream sundae. It will all be pretty much the same as what you were used to. The only difference is that your life is now more of a life of near solitude. It is a time for you to reflect and answer some questions about yourself. You need to learn who Peter is, to become, enlightened if you would.

Once you have achieved your knowledge, your job here is complete, and you can move on to your next phase."

This was all too much for Peter to handle. A sick feeling had settled into his stomach as he once again became overwhelmed by what was happening to him. The queasiness quickly turned to anger as he turned around and glared into her eyes.

"I'm ten! Why is all this…? I don't even know what you're saying right now! I'm ten! What do you mean enlightenment? A job? I'm ten! You want me to work a job?" Agitated, he started to pace around.

"Peter, please, you have to calm down," Miss Penntiworth said as the other people left the room.

Peter looked at her, amazed she could be so dismissive.

"Calm down!" he screamed. "You know I just lost my parents, right? I just lost everything in my life that was important to me! I don't care about your job! I don't care about you or this place! I want to go home!"

Hoping to get away from her, Peter ran down the hallway. He didn't know where he was going, but he had to get out of there. Maybe he could find a door that would lead him away from this awful place and take him home. Who was this woman? Why did she bring him here?

"Have I been abducted?" he asked.

He saw things on T.V. about this stuff, and his parents were always warning him about strangers. Or maybe this was another one of Bobby's games. Maybe he was trying to scare Peter and get his thrills out of making him cry? Maybe he was in a hospital bed and just imagining all of this. He remembered hitting his head, so perhaps that was what caused all of these hallucinations.

Then again, maybe this was a dream. That's what it had to be, a dream. Peter flung a door open and went back out to the courtyard. He ran over to an area covered with trees and, tucked away under the canopy, Peter found a corner nestled in the shadows. Here, he decided to slow down, sit on the ground, and take some time to try to figure everything out.

As he thought back through the day, Peter remembered going to his baseball game, and how he struck out and let his team down. He remembered Bobby chasing him and pelting him with rocks as he tried to get away. And finally, he remembered suddenly staring at the truck's bumper before he hit his head on the ground and everything went dark. From that point, the rest was a blur. This had to be a dream. Or at least his imagination.

His father had always accused him of having an overactive imagination, and maybe he'd been right. Then it dawned on him that, if this was a dream, he could try to wake himself up. It had happened before. He'd found himself in the middle of a bad dream and would force himself to wake up. Sometimes it worked and sometimes it didn't, but he definitely had to try. Peter began to scream as loud as he could. He pinched his arms, and at one point of desperation, he got up and ran over to a nearby drinking fountain. Peter held his face under the little cherub statue that was pouring water. Nothing worked, and his frustration grew. Thinking he must have missed some sort of detail, some tiny clue that would give him the answer he was looking for, Peter went back to his spot, sat down, and buried his face into his hands to think things through again.

"How do I wake up?" he whispered. "There has to be a way to wake up and get out of here."

He looked up and saw Miss Penntiworth standing in the courtyard, keeping her distance as she examined the leaves on the trees. He was still angry with her for what she said. Seeing her just made him angrier, so he got up and tried to run. Oddly enough, Peter kept running, yet everything looked the same to him. It was the same corner, the same drinking fountain. No matter how far or how long he ran, everything stayed the same. Even Miss Penntiworth stood in the same spot.

"What is going on?" he grumbled as his head starting to throb. "How do I stop this? How can I get away from here?"

He turned in a circle, fell back, and leaned up against the drinking fountain. Miss Penntiworth walked over slowly and kneeled down in front of him.

"Peter, I will always try my best to explain things to you, but you are going to have to help me. Some people, like you, have a more difficult time letting go than others. You have to have faith that what I tell you is actually happening. Right now, you are in denial, and I do not blame you at all. Do not feel bad if you're not enlightened quickly. Take your time. Take as much time as you need."

She stood up and looked around.

"This is actually a very exciting, very interesting place," she told Peter. "There's no rush for you to move on. Once you leave here, you are lifted to a different plane. You put everything you were behind you, and are presented with a beautiful afterlife."

These words made Peter wish he were home once again.

"But what about Mom and Dad? I can't be away from them. I don't want to be away from them." He felt as though he'd been punched in the stomach.

Miss Penntiworth put her head down.

"Your parents will get through this, Peter," she said softly. "It will be the most difficult tragedy they will go through in their lives, but they will get through it. I promise you that."

Lips quivering, Peter frowned, struggling to hold back the tears, but as the emotions flowed through him, so did the tears. Everything he loved had been taken away from him. Peter wanted nothing more than to wake up from this terrible nightmare in the warmth of his own bed, with his mom sitting next to him, rubbing his head and telling him that everything would be fine. What would have been his Halloween costume this year? How big of a Christmas tree would his father drag through the deep snow? These were things that Peter would never experience again, which made Peter so sick, sicker than he had ever felt before.

Miss Penntiworth led him over to a bench in the middle of the courtyard. There was a soft splashing sound coming from the fountain nearby which helped calm him down a little. Miss Penntiworth walked away, leaving him to take stock of his new situation.

The more he thought about being away from his parents, the more the ache in his stomach gripped at his insides. He sat there alone in the garden for some time, watching as Miss Penntiworth peeked out the window on occasion. As the time passed by, he wondered who else in that room today felt like he did. Everybody there seemed to be at ease with their recent news. Why was he the only one so upset? Why wasn't anyone else feeling this sick?

With all these questions running through his head, Peter couldn't help pacing around, trying to burn off some of his nervous energy. It didn't help. Peter felt more alone than he had ever felt before. At least back home, he could share his feelings with his mother and father, but here, he had nobody. Even though Miss Penntiworth seemed nice, this place could never be home, and he knew that's where he wanted to be. He paced as much as he could before he was too exhausted and sat down at the edge of the fountain to rest. That was when Miss Penntiworth walked up to him and gently put her hand on his shoulder.

"Come on, Peter. I will show you where you are staying," she said softly. "At least there you can be more comfortable as you try to come to terms with all of this."

He took a moment to stare at her and then looked around. He barely recognized the reflection he saw in the fountain. All of his life had been drained from his face as it sagged with sadness. At this point, it was useless to question what had happened. He was physically and emotionally exhausted. He took a deep breath and stood up. Miss Penntiworth went to put her hand on his shoulder again, but he pulled away. They left the courtyard and walked through a great hall toward a large stone staircase with an angel carved into each newel post. He kept looking around, hoping someone would jump out and yell surprise. Even though this would be one of the rottenest tricks ever, he'd welcome it wholeheartedly.

"If you remember that the staircase which leads to your room is adorned with two angels blowing their trumpets, you should be all right," she told him.

They climbed the stairs and took the first hallway to the left, which had a number of doors on both sides.

"Here we are," said Miss Penntiworth, pointing him down the hall. "Your room is the third door on the left."

She opened the door for him and, when he walked in, he noticed the room was larger than what he was used to back home. There was a large bed, a dresser, a writing desk, and a small potbelly stove set inside an old marble fireplace. The room had two windows, which brought in a bright, warm glow from the sun. He walked over to one of the windows and peered out.

Maybe something outside will help me figure out where I am, he thought.

He'd hoped to see a street sign, or a building name, something that would help him. However, all he saw was a large, unfamiliar forest. There were also snow-capped mountains in the distance that he'd certainly never seen in his hometown. Peter watched as several deer, antelope, and other smaller creatures, ran back and forth. He thought one of them was a pure white rabbit, but he wasn't sure. The rabbit hopped away, so he ran over to the next window, hoping to get a better look.

As he got to the window, he looked out, expecting to see the rabbit, but instead, he noticed tall waves from the ocean crashing up against the building. Confused, he stuck his head out the window and saw nothing but open ocean as far as the eye could see. Peter moved back to the other window only to see the forest still there. Nothing had changed except for the rabbit being gone. Again, he went back to the second window, and again, he noticed the ocean, but now there was a family of dolphins jumping in and out of the water. He turned to Miss Penntiworth with his mouth dangling open as he tried to comprehend what he'd just seen. She was facing away from him, adjusting a painting on the wall.

"It's nice to have different views, isn't it, Peter?" she asked, still focused on how level the painting was.

He didn't respond, and a frown appeared on her face. She turned around and walked over to his bed.

"Now, Peter, if there is anything you need, please, do not hesitate to ask. I want you to feel as though this is your home, and that we are family," she told him as she picked up his pillow and began to fluff it up for him.

Peter cringed at her words. He resented her for saying that. She was not family, and this certainly was not, nor would it ever be his home. He had literally been thrown into this situation.

She took one last look around, making sure things were in order.

"Everything you need, you will find here," she told him as she adjusted a mirror on the wall. "If you should have any questions, my office is right down the stairs."

She smiled at Peter as she left the room. All he could do was stare back at her, and then, once she'd left, he started to look around.

"The only thing that I am going to 'find' is a way out of here!" he snarled as he walked over to his bedroom door, slamming it shut.

Even though it seemed she was trying to make him feel better rather than upset him, the truth of the matter was, she'd failed. Peter was not at home, and he was certainly not with his family!

He walked over to the closet and opened the door. When he turned the light on, he nearly fell backward. This was HIS closet! All of his clothes were hanging there, and his toys and games were stacked neatly on the shelves, just as he'd left them.

"I wonder if…" he said as he reached behind one of the shelves.

Several years ago, Peter's mother and father went on a trip, so his grandmother came to stay with him. He was nervous about them leaving, so to help, his mother had given him a photograph of her and his father.

"Sweetheart, anytime you feel lonely or scared, just hold this picture really tight, and you will know we are with you always," her voice rang out in his head.

He smiled as he remembered what a comfortable feeling that photograph had given him. Peter reached behind the shelf, hoping that it would be there. His hand grabbed onto something, and as he pulled his hand out, he was relieved to see the picture of his mother and father smiling at him.

"Wait a minute," he said, somewhat puzzled. "How could this closet be the same as mine back home? Maybe I *am* just dreaming all of this!"

He walked over to the bed and sat on top of it. Peter's eyes grew wide as his room transformed itself into his room at home.

"This is unbelievable!" he yelped, looking around and watching all of his belongings appear before his eyes.

Not only were his posters hanging in the exact same place as they were back home, even his goldfish Happy was in his bowl swimming around. Peter jumped out of bed, but the room faded back to the way it was originally, wood-burning stove and all. Disappointed, he sat back down on the bed and the room once again transformed into his old room. Peter didn't want to move again, because as odd as all of this was, being in his old room made him feel better. He spent most of that day sitting quietly and looking around at his belongings. All the pictures on the walls, the curtains, even the sheets on the bed, were the same as the ones back home.

As dusk settled in, Peter lay back on his bed, motionless as he stared at his parent's picture.

"I wonder what they're doing right now," he mumbled. "Probably sitting down for dinner. I bet its meatloaf tonight."

His eyes started to glisten as he imagined some other kid taking his place at the dinner table. It used to be painful to carry on conversations with his parents at that table.

"What did you do in school today? Did you hang out with some friends? How is that new teacher?"

The questions were agonizing, and now in a room surrounded by silence, he longed to have them back. He remembered being home, lying in his room at night, the silence interrupted by the soft chimes of the grandfather clock downstairs in his father's office. As he looked at his room now, he knew there wouldn't be any clocks chiming any comfort for him. Nonetheless, Peter wasn't going to give in to this dream. He took another look at Happy swimming around and smiled.

"See," he said, "this is my room. Tomorrow, I will wake up, and Mom will be fixing me breakfast."

He got ready for bed and crawled underneath his sheets, adamant that everything would be different in the morning. As he lay there, looking up at the ceiling, he smiled, confident he was right, and as he closed his eyes, he kept repeating the same four words.

"This is a dream. This is a dream."

CHAPTER 2
It Will Never Be Home

When Peter woke up the next morning, he couldn't bring himself to open his eyes. He lay there perfectly still, listening intently for his mother, but when he didn't hear anything, he began to worry. Had he been wrong all along? Was none of it really a dream? The confidence that finally beamed from him yesterday was suddenly replaced by fear.

"Please, don't let this be true. Please, please don't let this be true," he kept whispering as he sat up in bed, his eyes still closed tightly.

It took everything in him to set his feet down on the floor. As he stood up from the bed, he still refused to open his eyes, hoping that when he did, the room would stay the same. Slowly, he stumbled over to the door, and once he'd gotten to it, he couldn't stop his hand from shaking enough to open it. He momentarily paused, pulled his hand back, and took a deep breath before trying again.

"Please," he whispered as he reached for the doorknob once more, his hand now wet with sweat.

This time he gently grabbed onto the doorknob, slowly turned it, and carefully pulled the door open. Even though he still couldn't hear his mother or father, Peter held on to the hope that it had all been a dream; he opened his eyes and quickly peeked around the door. Once he saw the ornate hallway he'd walked in last night, his chest felt like it weighed a thousand pounds. Peter slid down onto the floor and slammed the door shut.

"Why?" he cried out.

He buried his face into his hands as his whole body started to shake. His stomach felt as though he had swallowed a beehive; all the agitated bees stinging his insides until he was ready to erupt! He ran back to his bed and crawled underneath the sheets, hoping it would all go away.

All he could do was lie on his side and rock back and forth with tears streaming from his eyes.

"I want to go home. Please, I just want to go home," he whispered over and over again throughout the day until his mouth was too parched to speak.

As the days went by, Peter couldn't bring himself to leave his room. Each day Miss Penntiworth would come by, knock on his door, and patiently wait for him to break the silence. He, however, would never invite her in, nor did he even acknowledge her presence. They fell into a routine together. Eventually, she would give up and leave, but the longer she stood there, the more frustrated Peter became. At one point, he was tempted to shout at her to go away, to leave him alone, to never come back, but he vowed not to speak to anyone other than his parents.

Even though she was consistently ignored, this didn't discourage Miss Penntiworth. She was worried about Peter. Instead of standing in silence, she would eventually open his door and announce to him that she had brought him a meal. Day after day she would come into his room and leave a tray of food on the chest at the end of his bed. Day after day she would find him staring out his window or huddled up in his closet. Peter was not taking this well, nor was he expected to.

Several weeks had gone by without a response from him, until one day, Miss Penntiworth put the food down and decided to reach out to Peter, who was hiding in a dark corner of his closet. She walked up to it and leaned against the wall.

"Peter, dear," she said softly. "I know you're hurting inside. Please let me know when you're ready to come out of this room. There is nothing I can do to change this situation for you. There is nothing you can do, either. You need to come out of this room and continue on."

She waited for him to say something.

"I know you want to be with your family again, dear, and if I could do something about that, I would," she continued, hoping today would be the day he talked to her. "You have to realize, Peter, whether you like it or not, this is now your home. You will have to make the best of it."

Peter didn't move, nor did he bother acknowledging her. Nothing had been said for several minutes, and for a moment, he thought she'd given up and gone away.

"One day you will be reunited with your family Peter," she said, her voice startling him. "Until that day, you need to make a life for yourself.

And I hope you choose to have a happy life because it makes me sad to see you this upset and this miserable."

She stood there for another moment, waiting to see if he was ready to come out, but he didn't move. Miss Penntiworth walked away from the closet and stepped out of his room. As she left, she quietly closed the door, and the click of the latch let Peter know he was alone once again. The day passed by, and he continued to sit in the darkness of the closet thinking about what she had said, and how her words cut into him.

"She isn't my mother," he groused. "Who does she think she is giving me advice? She is not my mom! Only my mom can give me advice!"

He paused for a moment.

"Then again, I don't have a mother anymore," he reluctantly admitted to himself.

This thought caused his stomach to surge in pain, and he ran out of the closet and threw himself onto his bed, crying uncontrollably.

"Why can't I go home?" he screamed into his pillow. "Why can't I go home?"

Another day went by without Peter leaving his room. Throughout the day, he heard Miss Penntiworth outside his door listening to make sure he was getting by. In addition to this, she would also stop in and drop his meals off. However, he still wasn't eating much. Not only was his appetite affected by all of this, his sense of being was affected. He didn't know what time it was, or even what day it was, or how long he had been here for that matter. His routine continued to stay the same. He would wake up in the morning, hide in his closet thinking about his parents, and then cry himself to sleep at night.

The following morning, Peter walked over to the window, sat down in his chair, and looked outside. Off in the distance was an elderly man dressed in a yellow rain slicker and hat, sitting in a rowboat and casting his fishing line into the ocean. Peter sat there and stared at him for some time, lost in his thoughts. A soft knock broke the silence causing him to jump and turn towards the door.

"Peter," Miss Penntiworth said, peeking her head inside the room. "May I come in?"

As with every other day, he did not answer. He just turned back to the window and continued to watch the man fishing.

"Peter, dear, you need to talk about this," she said as she opened the door and stepped inside his room.

There was still no answer, and he refused to look at her.

"I am very concerned about you."

This caused a faint sniffle.

"I just want to go home; that's all I want," he finally said. "Please, let me go home. I miss my mom and dad. Please let me go."

"Oh, my dear, Peter," she said. "May I sit with you?"

Peter didn't answer. He continued to sit there, hoping Miss Penntiworth and everything else would go away. Instead, she brought a chair over to the window and sat next to him. They both stared out at the ocean, sitting there quietly for some time.

"Do you have any brothers or sisters, Peter?" she finally asked him, breaking the silence as she stood up and paced back and forth.

Peter shook his head.

"Well, when I was a little girl, my brother went off to war," she told him. "I was so sad. All I could do was cry uncontrollably as I watched him ride his horse Bucky away from our house. But before he left, he promised me he'd be fine and assured me he'd write a letter to me every week."

She stopped for a moment as she stared out the window and off into the distance.

"I loved him very much," she said as she looked down, and then she turned and smiled at Peter. "He kept his promise. Almost every week, I would receive a letter from him. One day, I got a letter, but it wasn't from my brother. The letter was from a close friend of his whom I knew. He wrote to tell me my brother was not going to be coming home. He also said my brother loved me very much and I should look out for my mother and my father."

She sat down next to Peter and took a brief moment to remember that time. After taking a deep breath, she turned to him.

"Peter, I was devastated," she said as she put her hand on top of his. "I didn't know what to do. My whole world felt as though it had collapsed around me. I never got to see him one last time. I never got to say good-bye to him, or tell him how much I loved him. I would have given anything to get my brother back home."

Peter looked at Miss Penntiworth and squeezed her hand ever so gently. She stood up and walked toward the window.

"I spent the next several months angry at my brother for leaving me, angry at my parents for letting him go, and angry at myself for thinking I'd let all of this time go by without getting to know him better. And do you know what I did?" she asked as she turned towards Peter.

Without looking at her, he shook his head.

"I shut down," she told him. "I closed myself off from the rest of the world."

Miss Penntiworth started to pace back and forth again.

"It was awful. I would not let anybody near me, nor would I speak to anyone about how I was feeling. Eventually, I became ill. So ill, that I was institutionalized. However, when I was at the hospital, I slowly began to speak to a nice doctor who would often check in on me. Over time, I started to feel more comfortable about opening myself up to this stranger. Believe it or not, I actually began to feel better. What I was holding inside was destroying me, but once I opened up and let go of my inhibitions, I was able to talk about the feelings I was having about my brother's death. It made me feel so much better," she said to Peter as she knelt in front of him. "I'm not saying you should be running up and down the halls celebrating. You should take time to grieve for yourself and for the loss of your family. But, Peter, I beg you please do not let your feelings consume you as I did. That does not help you and hurts you more. Find someone to talk to, anyone," she said as she sat down next to him again. "I would love for us to talk, but more importantly, I would just love for you to talk to anybody. Please, Peter, talk to somebody."

Sitting there for a moment, she waited for Peter to respond, but he didn't. He just sat there staring at the ground.

"I bet Mr. Grumsby would talk to you," she said as she gently nudged him.

Peter looked up and smiled.

"Take your time, Peter and when you are ready, I'm here to listen. If nothing else, try to have something to eat." She smiled and rubbed Peter's arm.

"You know, Peter, this place is quite fascinating. You can find many interesting things here, and you can also find the answers to most any question you come up with. I believe even a boy of your age would enjoy the adventures this place has to offer. You should give it a chance."

She smiled to him as she left the room, slowly closing the door behind her.

Peter stood up and walked over to his bed. He drew a heavy breath and sat on the edge of it, thinking about where he was, what Miss Penntiworth said, and what, if anything, he could do. After some time, he walked back over to his window and peered out. The little old man was pulling in the biggest fish Peter had ever seen before. He landed the fish into the boat, stood up to stretch out his back, and wiped the sweat from his brow. Then, almost instinctively, the man looked up and waved to Peter.

Somewhat surprised, Peter nodded to him, gave him a thumbs up, and went back to sitting on his bed. Seeing all of his things from home around him gave him some comfort. However, he still didn't enjoy spending all of his time in here. The room reminded him of home, but as such, it also reminded him of how much he missed home, especially his parents. Somewhat hungry, Peter remembered the tray of food Miss Penntiworth had left behind. He picked up the silver cover and underneath was a stack of chocolate chip pancakes drenched with butter and syrup. The smell was incredible, and his stomach started to grumble. He wasn't sure how long it had been since he'd eaten, nor did he really care. Food wasn't as important to him anymore, but he was hungry, so he sat down and quickly ate the stack of pancakes. When he finished his breakfast, he picked up the white linen napkin, wiped his mouth, and went back to staring out the window.

"Nothing has changed," he said. "Every day I wake up, and I'm here. This isn't a dream; it's a nightmare, but I can't just sit around and hope something changes. Maybe it's time for me to venture out," he added as he looked toward the door. "I'm not gonna find a way out of here from inside this room."

He then remembered what Miss Penntiworth said about being able to find answers to his questions. Maybe, outside his bedroom door, there was an answer for him on how to get home. He stood up and made his way over to the door, but when he got to it, all he could do was stand there and stare at the doorknob. In his mind, going out of his room meant he was accepting what had happened to him, and he wasn't sure he was ready to do that.

Nonetheless, he took a deep breath and put his quivering hand on the doorknob. With a quick twist of his wrist, he threw the door open. Peter stepped into the hall and, strangely enough, immediately began to feel better. After all, that time hiding, his room had become stale. It reminded him of the times he'd gotten punished by his parents and banished him upstairs, making his room more a prison than a paradise.

New surroundings might help him feel better. Probably not much better, but maybe better. He slowly stepped farther down the hallway and looked around. People were bustling all around. Nobody paid any attention to him, so he went down the stairs and found a door with a brass placard to the side of it.

"Beatrice Penntiworth" was etched into the metal.

The door was open, but when Peter didn't see her inside, he went in and waited. The office was warm and inviting, just as she was. It had a small writing desk behind two armchairs, covered with a floral-patterned fabric. There was a tiny calico cat curled up asleep on an overstuffed chair that was by the window, and a doily-covered couch in front of a fireplace warm with glowing embers. Every inch of the walls were covered with old photographs. Each was black and white and displayed in ornate frames; most of the pictures were of people standing next to Miss Penntiworth herself.

To his surprise, Peter saw a picture of Miss Penntiworth with someone who looked like Abraham Lincoln, and another person appeared to be Albert Einstein. He walked to the wall behind her desk and peered at a particular photo. In it stood a young girl with a great big smile on her face, and standing next to her was a boy not much older than Peter. He wasn't certain, but the girl looked like Miss Penntiworth. She had curly hair and wore a dress. In one hand she gripped onto the leg of a doll. In the other hand, she was holding the boy's hand. He was standing straight and tall, dressed in a military uniform, but he wasn't smiling.

"That must be her brother," Peter whispered.

"That is my brother," she said, startling Peter.

She walked up to the picture and adjusted it on the wall. "I'm very glad to see you, Peter. Please, won't you sit down?" she asked as she sat on the couch.

Peter nodded and took a seat next to her.

"I don't understand how I can be here," he quietly said to her. "I feel as I've always felt. I'm so confused."

"Oh dear, Peter, I am sorry all of this has happened to you," she told him. "But this is a wonderful thing. You now get the opportunity to become enlightened!" She told him, stretching her arms out in front of her.

He looked at her as though she was crazy.

"I don't want to be here, Miss Penntiworth! This is anything but wonderful!"

"I'm sorry, Peter. I did not mean to imply you should blindly celebrate your situation from the onset. Please, dear, by all means, challenge and confront what happens to you. Question the world around you. That is what life is. Whether you are living it back home, or here, that is life. However, once you do become enlightened, you get to move on," she told him as she leaned down and looked into his eyes.

He turned away quickly, afraid of what her eyes might show him this time. Even though he had no idea what she meant about becoming enlightened, it did sound like an opportunity to get home.

"So how do I become enlightened, and how quick can I do it?" he asked.

Miss Penntiworth smiled. "You know, I forgot how exciting life is through a child's eyes. Everything is new to you. Everything is there for exploration. So, by all means, continue to ask questions and investigate. Stay young in mind and in spirit, dear, because the longer you are able to look at the world through those wonderful young eyes of yours, the better. As a matter of fact, Peter, you should take some time today to get a feel for this place. Walk around and discover things. Tomorrow morning when you wake up, please come see me here in my office."

He sat there looking at her for a moment, waiting for an answer to his question, but he got the feeling an answer wasn't coming any time soon.

"Uh, sure, okay," he said, raising his eyebrows and slowly standing up. "Um, thanks, I think."

"Enjoy yourself!" she called out to him as he left the office.

"What the heck was that?" he muttered as he tried to figure out where to go or what to do.

If he wanted answers, he was going to have to go and find them for himself; most of his day was spent walking around and mumbling to himself.

"Maybe, just maybe, once I'm able to walk around this place with no questions, I can become enlightened, or whatever, and move on. If I can get out of here, maybe I can go home."

Even though he still didn't know what she meant by becoming enlightened, this gave him hope, a new outlook. He was going to make it his mission to find a way home, but for now, he agreed it was time to see what this place was all about. From what she'd told him, it sounded to Peter that the key to him getting home could be found somewhere in this building, and he had an idea of just where to start.

CHAPTER 3
Section III

Peter had spent most of the previous day roaming around, yet he couldn't find a way out of the building, nor did he find any answers to any of his many questions. As for today, it wasn't that he enjoyed getting up early, or that he was eager to start working, but he was determined to find a way home, and maybe the way to do that was by working this so-called job of his.

The sun had barely risen, and he wasn't sure whether Miss Penntiworth would be in her office when he got there, so he softly knocked before opening the door.

"My, aren't we an early riser?" she called out over the whistling steam from the copper teakettle she was holding.

"Would you like a cup, dear?"

"Um, no thank you," he said.

"Please sit down and make yourself comfortable. Give me a moment to finish making my tea, and we can start."

He walked over to the sofa and sat down. The calico cat he'd seen last time he'd wandered into the office was curled up asleep again in the corner. Woken up by the newcomer, the cat looked somewhat put out at having to share his spot with Peter.

"I'm not really sure what I'm supposed to do," he told Miss Penntiworth. "Am I going to go to school or something?"

She chuckled at this as she stirred a teaspoon of sugar into her tea.

"No, Peter. This is going to be a sort of learn-as-you-go experience. Let me try to explain. Heaven is an enormous place, and that place is made up of smaller sections. Almost like a staircase, you climb these sections until you reach your final destination. Everyone's destination is different, and you have some control over where you end your journey. However, before you continue your journey into the afterlife, you are given a temporary job, and once you fulfill the requirements of this job, you are entitled to move on, to take a vacation you might say," she said as she took a sip of tea from her cup and sat down next to him. "You see, Peter, during a person's life, they must at one time or another, have touched the lives of many others. People do this in different ways. They do it through their jobs, through some type of charity work, or some other way. There are many different ways to achieve this, but in your situation, because of your age and really through no fault of your own, you have not had a chance to do so."

"Since this is one of life's requirements, you were sent here to fulfill this requirement. This is what people like you do at the Conservatory. You might compare it to a sort of library. In the Conservatory, there are literally billions of books called 'LifeBooks,' and each of these books represents a person. Each workday you will be handling the books. Therefore, you technically become a part of that person's life by helping them get from day to day, and as such, you have the chance to touch many people's lives."

"Oh. Okay," Peter said, still unsure of what he was supposed to do. "Um, how long do I work at this temporary job?"

She stared up at the ceiling and pressed a finger against her lips.

"Oh, let me think." She paused for a moment, taking another sip of tea. "It really depends on the person, of course. However, most people usually finish up in about one hundred years or so."

Peter's mouth dropped open. All he could do was to sit there staring at her, unable to comprehend what she'd just told him.

"Peter, numbers like that do not mean as much here as they did before. Take myself, for example. I've been here for, I don't know, 380 or so years, and it just seems like just yesterday when I met Mr. Grumsby for the first time." She smiled. "I cannot recall if he was any happier that day, either."

Peter smirked at that.

"I know you may not think so, Peter, but believe it or not, he is one of the sweetest people I have had the pleasure to meet." She chuckled. "But promise not to tell him I said that."

Peter stared at her in disbelief. He couldn't fathom for a moment that anyone would ever describe Mr. Grumsby as being sweet.

"Well then, shall we go?" she asked as she stood up and covered her shoulders with a shawl.

"Um, sure, I guess."

They left her office and headed down the hallway, where they came upon another staircase. As they descended, it began to spread wider and wider. The light grew strong, and the warmth Peter started to feel enveloped him and made him smile. When they got to the bottom, they stepped into a wide-open room covered in bright red carpet.

"Alright, Peter, here we are," she said to him with a proud, beaming smile. "This is the Conservatory."

Peter and Miss Penntiworth walked into an immense round room capped with a rotunda covered in frescos. Looking up at the paintings, Peter thought they were some of the most beautiful things he'd ever seen. The frescos depicted a scene of angels looking down from the heavens onto a park where children were playing with their parents. In the center of the room was an immense white marble fountain. Seven winged angels blew water from trumpets into a circular pool. Large arched glass windows encircled the room, through which sunlight bathed the tropical trees scattered throughout, each of them filled with oranges, lemons, and grapefruit. Evenly spaced throughout was a series of wooden double doors, which towered above Peter. Between each section of doors, statues of different people stood about ten feet tall. Large oil paintings encased in golden frames hung on each side of the statues.

"This is one of the nicest rooms I've ever been in," Peter told her.

"Isn't it? We've been fortunate enough to have some very talented artists come through here over the centuries," she explained to him. "Each of them seems to enjoy leaving behind a beautiful example of their work."

Peter's head kept turning as they slowly walked past the large fountain.

"So, let me explain how this is going to work," she told him. "Your job is quite simple, really. Every other day you go to your section in the Conservatory. You take one of the LifeBooks from the shelf, open it, and remove the page marker. Once you've turned the page, you will replace the marker and put the book back into its place on the shelf. After that, you take the next book and do the same until you have completed your section."

She picked up a clipboard from a nearby table and flipped through several pages.

"Now, Peter, you are in section three, and your rows are 8237947 through 9952467. Follow me, and I will show you how to get there."

He followed her to one set of double doors. Above them, a glossy-wooden plaque engraved with III silently announced the room. The numbers were gilded in gold and hung prominently above them.

"I-I-I?" Peter questioned. "What does I, I, I stand for? Is this the pirate section?" he snickered. "Aye aye Captain," he said with a salute.

Miss Penntiworth looked at him with a dull expression in her eyes.

"Son, do you not know your Roman numerals?" she asked.

He stood there for a moment with his mouth hanging open. Being somewhat embarrassed, he closed his mouth, placed his hands in his pockets, and looked down.

"Of course, section three…Heh heh, don't I feel stupid?"

She just smiled at him. "Never mind that now, dear. Come on inside."

She struggled to push open one of the large wooden doors, which looked as though it weighed a thousand pounds. Just beyond was Section III, and as he stood there, Peter couldn't come up with any words that described what he was feeling. Section III didn't seem to end. Sunlight from leaded glass windows illuminated the never-ending rows of books that majestically stood over them and seemed to stretch for miles, disappearing into an abyss of marble and wood. Displayed in formation on these shelves were thousands upon thousands of books. Some were old, some new, some books were large, and others small. The leather covering these books had been tanned in all sorts of colors. The arrangement was a symmetrical nightmare. None of the books matched, yet they stood together, creating a beautiful, unified display.

For as many books as there were, it appeared there were that many people tending to them. People moved everywhere. Some carried stacks of books and placed them on the shelves, while others removed books and slid them into purple velvet wrappings, which were then aligned onto large wooden carts. People were climbing up and down tall library ladders, sliding back and forth along the metal rails affixed to the bookcases. And the carts, dozens of them, were pushed back and forth, in and out of the section. It reminded Peter of malls during Christmas shopping. But, unlike the chaos he'd witnessed there with his mother, here it was different. There was a system in place; everybody appeared to know what they were doing and were in a hurry to get it done. Peter was speechless. Miss Penntiworth stopped walking and turned to him.

"Well, here we are dear. These are the rows you will be tending to."

Peter looked at the bookshelves. Apart from the sign with the row numbers, the shelves looked like every other shelf. He figured there must have been at least ten thousand books in his section alone.

"As I explained, each of these books represents a person, and inside of them, their lives are laid out on each page. Take this one for instance," she said as she reached up to the shelf and pulled out one of the books.

It was a thick volume covered in heavy tanned blue leather.

"Roger Fangerstrum," she read from the cover. Then, she opened the book to where the pages had been separated by a blue silken page marker.

"Well, it looks as though Mr. Fangerstrum is going to retire from his job today."

Peter looked at Miss Penntiworth. She seemed to be in a haze, not blinking, just staring blankly at the pages. She spoke as though in a trance, slowly, with no inflection to her voice.

"Oh, how nice. His wife is surprising him with a 1960 Corvette, bright red, just like the one his father used to own. What a beautiful car." Miss Penntiworth shook her head and blinked rapidly several times. "Good for him."

She closed the book and gently placed it back into its position on the shelf.

"Please follow me, Peter," she then said as she ran her hands across the backs of several books in front of her.

He stopped for a moment and stood there, staring at the massive shelf.

"Why aren't these books ginormous? I would think that a page a day, three hundred and sixty-five days a year, carry the seven..." he said, trying to calculate the answer. "Anyways, wouldn't these books be huge?"

"Well, I guess that is all in one's perspective," she said.

"I don't understand."

"Peter, you are used to seeing how books look because of your school or library. You grew up accustomed to a certain way they looked and felt, so that is how you will see them here. In fact, this is how you will see everything here, in a recognizable form. This holds true of size, too. Up here, size does not mean the same as it would for you back home. Therefore, even though the size of an object is irrelevant, the appearance to you is, because you are accustomed to the way a book should look. Does that make sense?" she asked.

"Oh, sure," he said, rolling his eyes, even more, confused now than when he'd started. "So anyways, you were saying I have to turn ALL of these pages?"

"Yes," she replied. "However, you only have to turn them every other day. Each page is a day, so page one, day one, page two, day two. Well, you understand. Once day two is finished, you turn the pages to day three and four, and so on. As such, life goes on. Now, when you get to the end of a book, you lay the book on its side and leave it hanging slightly off the shelf. The end of the book means the end of the person's life. Another attendee will come along, take the book, and put it into a special cloth covering."

Miss Penntiworth walked over to a cart that had several books wrapped in purple velvet. She picked one up and took it out of the soft cover.

"Once the books are placed in their covering, the writing from the book is removed."

She opened it and flipped through a number of pages, all of which were blank.

"This book will now be used to write a new life story for someone else. I believe that is everything there is to know about the Conservatory. Do you have any questions for me?" she asked.

"Well, if I only turn these pages every other day, what do I do on the off days?" he asked.

"Well, you go and have fun, of course! You do whatever it is that a ten-year-old boy would do. You can walk around and explore. You do whatever makes you happy. Whatever you want."

Peter walked over and took a book off one of the shelves. He turned the book around so he could see each of the sides. There didn't seem to be anything special about it; it looked like any other book he'd ever come across in his life.

"Miss Penntiworth, what would happen if I turned the pages ahead to see what's going to happen?" he asked.

She smiled at him.

"Peter, you are as inquisitive now as when you were back at home. Everyone is curious, nosy, interested, whatever you want to call it, and it is perfectly normal to feel that way. Quite frankly, it is expected. If you want to know what happens to a person in their book, then, by all means, look ahead."

His heart raced when he thought about finding a book belonging to a major-league baseball player, or someone he knew, but he also felt apprehensive.

"What happens to the person whose book I'm reading? Won't they get all goofed up?"

Miss Penntiworth chuckled. "Well, I'm not exactly sure what you mean by all goofed up, but, have you ever had a premonition?"

"A premon–" he stumbled to say.

"It is the equivalent to looking ahead in your life. Have you ever had an occasion where you were someplace and felt like you knew you were going to be there? Or maybe there was a time you remembered a dream you had, and what you dreamed about actually came true."

Peter nodded his head.

"People have them all the time," she told him. "They feel they knew something was going to happen. What they don't know is these occurrences are caused by us when we look forward in that person's book. The person will usually dismiss this feeling and not give it another thought. So don't worry, dear, it's harmless. In the Conservatory, helpers like you look because they become curious with other person's lives, so they read ahead. This causes the person they are reading about to have a premonition. Then there is something called déjà vu. That's the feeling a person has when they feel they've already been somewhere before, or have done something that seems familiar. This happens when the library helpers read the previous pages of a person's book."

"Interesting." He nodded as he put the book away.

"Now, let's continue our tour, shall we?" she asked as they walked out of the Conservatory. "There are a couple more places you need to know about."

As they walked down the halls, Peter looked around, still amazed at how large this place was. There were doors everywhere, and the halls seemed to never end. However, Peter was starting to get bored. That was until Miss Penntiworth turned down a hallway that was darker than the rest. The only light came from the flickering candle sconces adorning the walls. Each of the other halls Peter had been in had windows, whether stained glass or clear and had crystal chandeliers illuminating the way. There were also paintings on the walls, carpets on the floors, and statues and vases decorating every other inch of this place.

This hall, however, had none of that. The chipped and peeling walls of pale-gray plaster, cracked by years of neglect, turned away any curious explorers. Other than the sconces, which themselves were old and rusted, the hall was plain and empty. Almost as though they were headed to a spooky dungeon, a fact which piqued Peter's curiosity.

Miss Penntiworth stopped in front of a door that looked like it belonged guarding the entrance to a castle. There were wide wooden planks gripped together with two iron braces spanning the door. The handle of the door was a hefty circular piece of pitted black iron.

"Ah, here we are," she said. "Now, Peter, it's important we remain quiet. If you want to talk, please do so by whispering."

She slowly twisted the huge iron handle and opened the door into a room even darker than the hall.

"This is the Nabi's room," she whispered as she walked in and quietly closed the door behind them.

The cold air immediately hit Peter.

"Who are the Nabi?" he whispered, able to see his breath form a cloud before him.

"The Nabi are the keepers of the LifeBooks. They create them by inking the lives of the people who are later named on the covers. As they write upon the pages, a day in the life of that person is created. Once the book is finished, a name appears on the cover."

"How do they know what to write?"

"Well actually, Peter, they don't," she explained to him. "The Nabi have no control over the writings. It's almost like breathing. There is no thinking on their part when they are writing; they simply write what's inside of them at that time. The words almost, you might say, pour from their quills onto the pages."

Peter tried to look around, but the room was too dimly lit. The candles flickering throughout the room caused shadows to dance across the gray, granite slab floor. They were the only things in this room that appeared to have some sort of life to them. The only other light in the room came from jars set on the tables in front of something that must have been these Nabi she was talking about. There was no sound in the room other than an incessant scratching.

"What is that annoying noise?" he asked her.

"The scratching noise? Those are the quills the Nabi use to write in the LifeBooks."

As he moved through the room, Peter noticed a stench lingering in the air that made him only want to take short puffs of breath. It was like being in a damp, musty basement. Peter didn't like the feeling of this room and wasn't sure whether he was shivering from the cold or from the fear.

Through what little light there was, he could see three long wooden tables situated one right in front of the other. The walls around him were made of large stones with sporadic patches of moss growing on them. There were no windows, and the room truly reminded Peter of a dungeon. It was really quite an eerie place.

As Peter drew closer to one of the tables, he jumped back, startled by what he saw. At each table sat thirteen of these so-called Nabi. They were hunched over, scribbling in the books lying in front of them. Each of the Nabi was covered in a brown, hooded cloak. The eeriness of the room paled in comparison to the Nabi. Their eyes were cloudy white orbs with no pupils. Their faces were sunken deep into the hoods of their cloaks, barely illuminated by the candles sitting before them.

As best as Peter could tell, the Nabi didn't appear to be alive. They looked like grotesque statues. The only sign of movement was their hands scratching across the pages of the books that were in front of them. He watched as the Nabi followed the same routine: they dipped their quills into the ink jars, wrote several lines in the books, and then again and again and again; they'd start the routine all over. They did not look up, they did not stand, they did not speak. They just sat there, dipping their quills and scratching sentences across the amber colored pages of the books.

The ink was a brilliant gold color that shined brighter than the candles in the room and illuminated the Nabi's lifeless faces. Peter glanced curiously at the books. He slowly walked closer to one of the tables and stretched his neck to try to look over the shoulder of one of the Nabi. Frightened by the way they looked, he was hesitant to get too close to them, but his curiosity got the best of him, and he had to see what the books were.

When Peter was within a hand's reach to one of the Nabi, he stepped back for a moment. They were the foulest things he had ever smelled. It was a mix of wet dog and a musty, moldy old blanket. Peter pinched his nose and drew close again. As he looked over the Nabi's shoulder, his attention was now focused on its' hand, which was holding a quill. The skin of its' hand hugged tight to the bones. So much so, that Peter could make out each individual bone in its' fingers. Their skin was a grayish white color that reminded Peter of a dead fish he'd seen on the beach once.

When the Nabi wrote, the words didn't appear right away. Once the quill was dipped into the ink, the previous sentence scribed itself across the page. The brightness of the ink projected the words against the pale white skin on the Nabi's face. As the ink dried, it turned from a bright gold to a deep black. Peter was fixated as he watched.

Even though he stood next to them, the Nabi barely gave him the attention a fly on the wall would receive. Once they were finished with a book, they would place their quill on the table and sit perfectly still, staring off into the distance. After several moments, a helper entered the room, closed the cover of the completed book, and then took it over to a cart, which had dozens of other books on it.

"What happens to the books on the cart?" Peter asked Miss Penntiworth.

"Once the cart is full, another helper will come in and take the books to the Conservatory so they can be placed on the shelves," she whispered.

Another helper came into the room and approached the table where the Nabi had finished. She picked up the empty ink jar and replaced it with a full one. Shortly after that, another helper arrived with a new book. He placed it down on the table in front of the Nabi and gently opened the cover. The Nabi snapped out of his trance, picked up the quill, and continued to write. It was all somewhat fascinating to Peter. He sat there quietly watching the process until Miss Penntiworth broke the silence.

"They have no emotion for what they are writing," she told him. "They do not feel excitement or sadness for what is about to happen to the person they are writing about, nor do they embellish on what is to be written. It is just written."

"Why don't they talk?" he asked. "They just sit there. Not even a hello. I don't even think they know we're in the room."

"They know we're here, Peter. They sense life; they actually long for life. However, their existence is a sad one."

Peter stopped staring and looked at her.

"Why is it so sad?" he asked.

"Many good things happen in a person's life, which are written in these books. However, many bad things happen, as well. Would you want to be the one to write that a husband and father is shot on the street as their spouse is preparing their anniversary dinner?"

He knew exactly what she was talking about.

"Why would anyone want to do this job? Who would make someone sit here and do this?" he asked.

"Well, Peter, it's not quite as simple as someone making someone else do something. The Nabi picked their own destiny. It does take a special someone to do what they do for eternity. That's what the Nabi are for. They start off like you and me. They were once in human form, living their lives every day, like everyone else. The problem is they gave up their gift. They gave up on life, and ended it prior to when it was supposed to end."

"You mean they killed themselves?"

"Yes, I do, Peter. And as such, they are now required to spend eternity writing the lives of others. Their atonement for their actions is to indirectly live what they gave up on. So they write about people having fun and being with loved ones. They witness the pain a person goes through when a loved one passes. That is why their existence is a sad one. Over time, their eyes glaze over white so that they are blind to the words on the page."

Peter wasn't sure whether to feel sorrow or anger for the Nabi.

"Why is it so cold in here?" he asked as a shiver ran up his arms.

"It is cold in here because there is no warmth of love or compassion other than the words written in those books. Everything goes into those books. The warmth, the moods, the feelings, the life, nothing is left here in this room. It all goes into the books," she said.

Miss Penntiworth adjusted the shawl on her shoulders and nodded her head toward the Nabi.

"This is why the Nabi have no feelings. It is better for them not to. If they did, they would be driven mad by what they write."

Peter couldn't believe it.

"What an awful way to live," he said. "Who would want to live like that?"

"Peter, there are things far worse than a life without feelings," she told him. "Think about the people that the Nabi left behind. People who now live their lives day after day asking why this person would have left them behind, wondering if there was anything they could have done to prevent it. Some of them blame themselves for what that person did. It is the ones left behind who live with the pain and the suffering from these actions. In a way, the Nabi have gotten off easy compared to the turmoil they've left behind. I do not begrudge them for their actions. However, I do not pity them, either."

The thought of his parents' sadness caused Peter's heart to ache. He wondered how much pain and turmoil his family was going through without him. Miss Penntiworth led him away from the Nabi and over to a corner of the room.

"Also, remember this Peter, the Nabi are to be revered, for they have great powers," she said. "They could become evil from the powers they hold over mankind. The Nabi could stray from their tasks and write things which should not be written."

Peter was now starting to shiver uncontrollably as the cold in the Nabi's room grew.

"Why don't we continue on with our tour?" she suggested. "We don't want to disturb the Nabi any further."

They walked out of the room, and Miss Penntiworth shut the door behind them. It felt good to be back in the hall where Peter could get warm again, and as soon as they entered the next hall, everything got brighter. He felt better now that there were windows, sunlight, and warmth again. They walked up to a door that had light struggling to escape from underneath and through the cracks in the wood. Miss Penntiworth took out a black iron ring from under her shawl, which had several old keys on it. This was the only time he ever saw her unlock a door. Once she opened it, Peter shielded his eyes from the brilliant light pouring into the hallway. When his eyes were finally able to adjust, he noticed that behind the door was a small room. They both walked inside where several shelves lined the walls. On them, meticulously positioned in neat little rows, were thousands and thousands of the ink jars the Nabi used.

"Why is this ink so bright?" he asked, still squinting from the glow.

Miss Penntiworth walked over to him.

"The ink from these jars glows like the sun, for that is the life that fills them. Life is a bright light on the dark emptiness, similar to what the Nabi's room represents," she said as she pointed down the hall towards the Nabi's room. "All emotion, any sense of life, is collected on those pages in the LifeBooks. There is nothing left to waste."

She picked up one of the ink jars and showed it to Peter.

"You see, Peter, each of our lives is connected to one another. You only have to see the ink pens the Nabi use to prove that. As the last word on the last page is written, a minuscule amount of ink is left behind on that pen. There is no getting past it, ink will be left on the pen no matter how small the amount, but the pen is never wiped clean. As I stated before, every drop of ink is valuable because it is life, therefore, it is never wasted. I cannot imagine the pens being wiped clean prior to the start of the next book because that precious, albeit small, bit of life would be wasted."

"Once the next book is started, the pen is dipped into the new ink jar. The ink from the previous jar is mixed with the ink from the new jar. Old meets new, and one life is connected to the next. Therefore, all of us are connected to each other. Do you understand?" she asked.

"Sort of," he said.

"Well, do you recall the story with the nice man who stayed in his hometown so he could look after his father's business? What was the name of that?" she asked as she stared toward the ceiling and tapped her finger against her lip. "Well anyways, that's not important. What is important is that the man was visited by a very nice angel who showed him what life would be like if he had never been born. The man did not realize how many lives were affected and changed by his birth. Take, for instance, the man's brother. Not only was his brother's life altered, but also the lives of any person who ever associated with that boy, and the string continues."

He still seemed confused, so she put the ink jar back onto the shelf and led him outside into a small courtyard.

"Let me show you an example, Peter," she said as she walked up to one of the dozens of fruit trees in the courtyard.

The tree was filled with large red apples. Peter grabbed one and started to eat it.

"Take this apple tree, for instance," she said to him. "If it is watered and cared for properly, all of the apples flourish and become delightful tasty fruit."

As she spoke, all of the apples grew to an enormous size. The branches bowed, and the bark creaked from the weight of the now pristine fruit.

"If anything is altered – no water, no fertilizer, little sunlight, for instance – not only one apple suffers, but all are affected."

With that said, all of the apples on the tree shriveled up and turned brown, including the one Peter was holding.

"You see, what happens to one, in this case, the tree, affects the whole, all of the apples."

"Oh, I see," Peter said as he now started to realize her meaning. "It's almost like dominoes: Where one is knocked down, it knocks down all of the others."

"Exactly, Peter," she said. "That is very perceptive of you."

The tree returned to normal as they walked back into the hall. After Miss Penntiworth locked the room, they continued their tour.

"Now fate is final, and it is exact," she continued. "As I explained to you earlier, once the books are placed into the purple velvet wrapping, the writing in them is erased, and the pages are cleared. The books are then placed in a storage room until they are needed by the Nabi. Once the Nabi start to write in these books, the ink will only last as long as there are pages in the book, no more, no less. Boy, girl, tall, short, it is uncertain whose life will be written in a particular book. Fate directs how thick the book is, and which ink jar is used for that book. The thicker the book, the longer a person lives."

They both stopped in front of her office.

"Well, it is getting late, Peter. Tomorrow is an off day, so you have the whole day to enjoy your time and explore. Come on, I will take you back to your room now. Do you have any questions?" she asked.

Peter shook his head. There was only one question on his mind: Was he ever going to be able to go home? But he knew Miss Penntiworth wouldn't, or couldn't, answer it for him. Even though he'd started to find out how this place worked, he still didn't have an answer. It was going to be up to him to find a way out and get back home to his parents. Peter wasn't sure how long it had been since he was last with his parents, he knew it had been too long; but he also knew, deep down in his heart, that this would all end tomorrow.

CHAPTER 4
A Door in the Woods

No matter how long Peter was stuck in the Conservatory, it never failed. Every morning when he woke up and saw his room, his heart would burst with excitement. Unfortunately, as soon as his feet hit the floor, the cold stone walls would reappear and remind him of where he was. It was the same routine every morning, never wanting to admit, refusing to believe; Peter fought his situation. When the subtle anger inside him dissipated, he would sit there momentarily, staring at the picture of his mom and dad, and swear a promise to go home to them.

He spent the next several hours walking down one hallway after the next. It reminded him of some of the museums his parents would drag him to. They were all very large, very pristine old buildings with a bunch of stuff in it he couldn't care less about. This place had a lot of the same types of statues and artwork. Most of his day was spent walking past several small gardens, and dozens of doors that he opened, but they didn't take him anywhere he was interested in going.

"I've been at this for hours and haven't found a way out," he said on yet another day of mindless wandering.

Frustrated, he looked around for a new direction to go, finally going back to some of the gardens he'd passed to see if any of them led away from the building. He remembered passing a specific garden, one with a pond and a clump of trees. "Maybe this will take me somewhere," he said, opening the glass door leading to it.

Once he walked out the door, he was immediately overcome by the smell of flowers and fresh cut grass. A soft breeze rustled his hair. Looking up into the beautiful blue sky, he watched as a puffy white cloud slowly drifted by.

"Boy, does it feel good to be away from that place," he said as he took a deep breath of fresh air.

The pond up ahead looked like the perfect place to sit for a moment. The breeze washing over him was so relaxing that he decided to rest for a moment. After all of this time, he finally had a moment where he felt at ease, and it was a welcome relief from all of the stress and anxiety he'd been feeling up until now.

A splash from a fish jumping out of the water woke him.

"What the heck?" he said as he quickly stood up and tried to figure out how long he'd been asleep. "I hope it isn't going to get dark soon."

The sun was barely above the trees, so Peter rushed toward the woods, but his grumbling stomach caused him to pause. Fortunately, Peter found himself standing in the middle of a field covered in blackberry and raspberry bushes. They were the largest, juiciest, berries he'd ever seen. Since he missed breakfast and wasn't even sure whether or not he'd missed lunch, Peter decided to stuff himself full of the delicious fruit. Once he was nice and full, Peter continued walking over to the woods where he found a dirt path disappearing deep into the forest. Feeling somewhat adventurous, he entered the forest.

This forest seemed no different from any other forest he'd been in. Along the way, he saw some deer, raccoons, and several other animals, some he recognized, and some he didn't. None of the animals appeared to be dangerous, so he continued on his journey, crossing over a small wooden bridge on top of a twisting stream before taking a moment to stop and rest. Off in the distance, he could hear a dull, roaring sound.

"What's that noise?" he wondered.

He walked to the other side of the bridge to get a better look, and after peeking through the thickets of brush, Peter saw a tall waterfall obscured behind a tree line. Wanting to get closer, he took a branch from a nearby tree and used it as a sword to cut a path through the overgrown foliage.

"Maybe this stream will lead me away from here," he said as he panted and swung his crudely fashioned tool.

Once he got through the brush, he saw the waterfall fell into a small lake. It had been a long day, and he was hot. The lake looked so cool and refreshing that he took off his socks and sneakers just before sticking his feet in. The water felt terrific, so good in fact that Peter took a moment to go swimming. After taking his shirt off, he jumped in and swam over to the waterfall. He remembered reading a book where there was a secret cave behind a waterfall. Curious, he swam through the rushing water, but unfortunately, there was nothing there but a solid granite wall.

The sun was slipping behind the trees: it would be dark soon. He swam back, got out of the water, and got dressed. Swimming around was fun, but it wasn't getting him home. After finding his makeshift sword and fighting his way back to the path he'd been on, he continued forward. It was getting later, and he was exhausted. He quickly looked around for a place to lie down and rest for the night. Tomorrow morning, he would continue on, refusing to step foot back inside that building. The trees and the foliage were too thick in the area he was in, but nearby, there was a path leading up a small hill. Perhaps there would be a place on top of the hill where he could set up a crude camp.

As he made his way to the top of the hill, he saw an opening in the woods, but abruptly dropped his stick and froze. Just beyond the opening was an oddly placed glass door, framed on either side by shrubs and thickets too dense to see through. He approached it cautiously.

What in the world was a door doing out here? he wondered as he opened it and stepped inside.

Peter found himself in a hallway, much like all of the other halls he had been in earlier. He stood there for a moment, trying to figure out where he was.

"Wasting your time, I see, boy."

That voice! Peter recognized that voice. He turned around just in time for Mr. Grumsby to push past him. Mr. Grumsby barely took the time to scowl at him before continuing down the hall and disappearing behind a door.

Peter had been walking for hours! There was no way he could still be back in the Conservatory! He looked back out the door and saw the forest beyond. Of course, he couldn't see the bridge or the lake through all of the trees, but it was definitely the same forest. He turned around and ran down the hall Mr. Grumsby had just come from. A short time later, he found the large fountain, a sign he was close to his own room.

This is impossible

He retraced his footsteps and returned to the door where his journey had begun so many hours ago. The pond where he took a nap was still there. Just to make certain, he walked out the door and looked up. Night was falling, and the sky was turning a deep shade of purple. The crickets were chirping quietly in the distance, and there was a crispness in the air which reminded Peter of autumn nights back home. He walked back into the hallway, thoroughly confused, but he was too tired to try to figure this out. It was his first day of work tomorrow, so he abandoned his escape plan and opted to get some sleep.

"Not so fast boy." Mr. Grumsby had reappeared and was now behind Peter with his ear pressed up against the wall. "Put your hand here."

Peter looked at Mr. Grumsby, shrugged his shoulders, and walked over to the wall.

"What does this feel like?"

Peter put his hand on the wall and looked at Mr. Grumsby.

"Rock?"

"No wise guy, press harder."

"Cold rock?" Peter tried.

Mr. Grumsby's visor tilted downward. "Whatever they see in you is beyond me. Come over here."

They walked over to another section of wall. Mr. Grumsby started to massage the stone. "Ah yes, here we go. What does THIS feel like?"

Tired and bored, Peter slumped over to where Mr. Grumsby stood. He slowly raised his arms and felt the wall again. "Um, I don't know, a different kind of stone?"

"Ugh. Wrong again. Concentrate. Try to imagine your hand being pushed through the stone."

Again, Peter tried. He focused as best as he could.

"Shut your eyes and imagine your hand melting into the wall." Mr. Grumsby told him.

Peter did as he was told, and just as he was beginning to fall asleep, he felt a small jolt of electric ripple through his hand. It felt as though he grabbed a hold of a cactus. He jumped back and looked at his fingers.

Mr. Grumsby's eyebrows raised.

"Well, what do you know? Maybe this can work," he said before he hurried down the hall.

CHAPTER 5
A Mysterious Mist

After gorging himself full of berries the previous day, Peter wasn't very hungry in the morning. Before he did anything else, he promptly made his bed, which caused him to smile. He remembered when his mother would scold him for not doing this, and as he tucked his blanket in, he fondly thought about her. In the past, it was always a mundane chore he wasn't eager to do, and would often try to skip. Now, it was a cherished reminder of his mom, and he actually looked forward to doing it each day. He took the photograph of his parents from his nightstand and put it back into its special hiding place in the closet before he left the room.

When he got down to Section III, it was packed with people rushing past him pushing carts and carrying books. He stood there in awe. Even though it had only been a day, he'd forgotten how immense this place was. There were more books in front of him than he thought he would ever see in his entire life.

"Well, I guess I need to get going," he said, taking a deep breath.

He grabbed a ladder perched up against the shelves and slid it over to the beginning of his section. After reaching the top rung, he removed the first book. It was not a very large book, so he opened it on top of the ladder and turned the page, carefully replacing the silk page marker. He closed it and put it back on the shelf. It took about thirty or forty books before he finally got bored. So bored, his mind began to wander.

What do I need to be here for? he thought as he stepped down from the ladder. *Let some adult worry about this. I can be outside exploring or doing something that kids do around here.*

Peter left the ladder where it was and scurried out of his section, excited to continue on with his explorations of this new place. He went from room to room, peeking in doors and going up and down different stairs. The one thing he couldn't find was a door that truly led him far away from here. Oh sure, he'd been in several courtyards. One even had an impressively large fountain with three dolphins spitting water into a pool, which of course he took time to splash around in. Another courtyard had a variety of fruit trees. It was here that Peter spent a good amount of time filling his face with apples and oranges. Yet another had a bunch of flowers and plants all neatly aligned in rows. His mother loved flowers. He thought of her fondly as he walked through that one.

"She always liked to garden," he said as he picked one of the daisies.

Out of all of the doors he'd encountered and opened, none of them led to what he assumed was the outside of this immense building.

What does the outside of this place look like? Will I ever find a freakin' door that gets me out of here? he thought, slamming yet another failed door shut.

His feet dragged as he stared at the floor and wondered whether he was in a castle, or maybe it was like the airport he and his parents had flown from when they went to Europe? Perhaps it was a big warehouse. He'd spent most of the day looking around, forgetting all about his section and his task of turning the pages of the LifeBooks.

Hoping for better results, Peter tried one more door before giving up for the day. As he opened it, he walked into a large living room with floral patterned couches and chairs. Curtains covered the windows, and doilies adorned the tables. A fire was crackling in the fireplace, and seated on one of the couches was Miss Penntiworth, sitting quietly, reading a book.

"I trust you are enjoying your tour?" she asked Peter.

How did she know what I was doing? he wondered.

Peter didn't know what to say. She looked up from her book and slid her glasses down to the end of her nose.

"Come in, Peter. Please, have a seat over here, son."

She slid over far enough for Peter to sit down next to her. The fluffy cushions enveloped him. He felt so comfortable.

"Would you like a cookie, dear?" she asked, handing him a plate of warm, gooey chocolate chip cookies.

His mouth watered at the sight of them.

A cold glass of milk would make this complete, he thought.

Reaching for a napkin on the table next to him, his hand bumped into a cold glass of milk.

"Now this is Heaven," he said as he sat back and took a sip of milk.

"Peter, let me explain how things work here, and what happens when things don't work here. Now I know it is a huge assumption on our part that a boy of your age can know how important something is that is so boring to him. But you see Peter, if you do not turn the pages of all those books, nothing happens in those lives. If their lives cannot move forward, nobody else's lives can move forward."

"Who would know?" he asked.

"Well, for one thing, imagine a person such as yourself in a section of library similar to yours. Let's say that helper climbs that big ladder and reaches for that huge heavy book on the topmost shelf. They drag it all the way down to the table because it is just too big to hold up there on that ladder. Now Peter, this poor soul lays this book on the table and opens the large, dusty cover, just so they can turn that one lonely page. One page, out of a million pages, just so they can drag that book all the way back up the ladder. Now, what do you suppose happens when they turn that page and the page drifts back from where it was. I would think that it was a fluke and the wind must have blown it back, wouldn't you?" she asked him.

"Sure," Peter said.

"So here they are turning that page again, eager to get on with their job. Alas, the page is turned, and it returns back to its original spot. They try again, and again, and the page turns back over and over again. Can you imagine how frustrating, and maybe even infuriating that would be? Especially if the person is someone like Mr. Grumsby."

"Of course," Peter responded softly with a mouth full of crumbled up cookies.

"Well, dear, that is exactly what happens when one person here decides it is not worth the trouble of turning a page. If all of the pages in all of these books are not being turned at one time or another, then nothing moves forward. Remember when I told you about déjà vu?"

"Days of who?" he asked.

"No, Peter, déjà vu, when a person has the feeling they have done something already or have been somewhere before."

"Right, yes, I remember."

"In actuality, this happens when the pages in the LifeBooks are not turned. So in reality, those people are actually living that moment again. What starts off as déjà vu, turns into the same day repeating itself over and over until that page is turned."

Peter paused for a moment.

"Now let's take all of that out of this equation, Peter. Do you know how important the Conservatory is? Or how important the LifeBooks are, and what is inside of them, how important those pages are? Think about it for a moment. Think about what is important to you. What would cause you great concern if something didn't happen?" she asked him. "Maybe one of those pages could be a great cartoonist creating the next immensely popular comic strip. Peter, that one little page, in a sea of so many other pages could have a doctor who is about to find the cure for cancer."

All of a sudden, Peter felt as though the cookie in his mouth was a thousand times larger and impossible to swallow.

"Everybody must be really ticked off at me," he mumbled through the crumbs.

There he was, wandering around and exploring, not realizing he was holding up a bunch of other people. He just sat there moping, until Miss Penntiworth put her hand on his shoulder.

"Peter, I am not telling you not to have fun. You are a child, I realize that, but you have to remember that part of the reason you are here is to turn the pages in all of those painstakingly boring books, as you consider them."

"Sorry," he said, his head hanging low.

"Don't be sorry, dear," she told him. "Just understand and appreciate what I am saying to you. Now, put a cookie in each hand of yours and be on your way."

Peter smiled at her, took two cookies, and left the room. He walked down the hall, trying to remind himself how important it was for him to turn the pages of those books. It was a boring task, sure, especially for a kid like Peter, but he had to put those thoughts out of his head.

Maybe I can make some sort of game out of it. he pondered. *Or maybe I can read part of the book to see what these people are up to. That could be interesting, and maybe even fun unless I find an old math teacher or something.*

The last thing he wanted to do was spend the day watching someone teach math problems.

When Peter finally made it back to his section, he finished the last bit of cookie and stood there staring at the large doors with the three I's above them.

"Stay focused," he told himself as he took a deep breath and pushed the heavy doors open.

After what Miss Penntiworth said, Peter didn't want any distractions. He walked through Section III without paying attention to what anybody else was doing. Even Mr. Grumsby, who was standing quite still, his ear pressed up against a wall, with one hand resting high over his head and one hand low toward the floor didn't sidetrack him. Peter just shook his head and continued on. He made his way over to his shelves and stood there, staring at all of the books. He'd forgotten what a daunting task he had before him.

Peter was unable to move as he became overwhelmed.

"This is what I'm destined for?" he reluctantly asked, but he refused to let it get to him. He stuck his chest out, walked up to the shelf where he left off and took the next book off it.

He couldn't tell why this book was so special. It was like any other book he remembered seeing in his school library. Carrying it over to a nearby desk, he laid it down and opened it. The pages were made from thick, heavy paper, and the writing was pristine calligraphy. A purple silk ribbon rested in the spine of the book and kept the pages separated. The words flowed straight and smooth across the unlined pages. After carefully picking up the page marker, he draped it over the top of the book and slowly turned the page. Unsure what to do next, Peter examined it further before flipping forward through a series of pages. Not too impressed, Peter began to read the first line.

"A son is born to a loving couple," it read, and as Peter stood there, a cloudy white mist cascaded from the pages of the book onto the floor where he stood.

As it bounced off the floor, the mist began to swirl like a tornado, up and around him, making it impossible to see through, so he frantically tried to wave it away. Once it cleared, Peter looked around and was glad to see he was still in his section. He cautiously began to read the words again, and again, the mist spilled from the pages of the book and surrounded him in a swirling vortex. This time he didn't wave it away. Several minutes passed and, when the mist dissipated, the library section had transformed into a hospital delivery room.

Peter slammed the book shut and tried to catch his breath. His eyes were wide, and suddenly, he was transported back into his section.

"Wow! This is amazing!" he said as he opened the book again and started to read once more.

Just as before, the mist formed around him, and he found himself standing in the middle of the hospital room. Doctors and nurses walked past, yet they weren't paying any attention to him. A deep, bellowing voice echoed off the tile floor as it narrated the sentences in the book.

"The first child of this relationship has been born. He is eight pounds, four ounces, and has a patch of black hair."

Peter walked up to the bassinet, resting closely beside the hospital bed. He looked inside and saw a little baby boy smiling up at him.

"Well, look at you," he said. "You have the same color hair as me."

The baby giggled and reached for Peter.

"Hey. You also have three freckles by your left eye like I do," Peter said as he smiled and reached forward to touch the baby.

The little boy went to reach for Peter's finger before he became distracted by his mother's voice.

"What are you doing, sweetheart? Are you stretching your arms?" she cooed to the infant.

Peter thought the mother had seen him, but then realized he was invisible to her as well. He stood there for a moment and then smiled at the baby.

"Man do they get specific," he said.

Peter waved good-bye to the baby and found himself back inside his section of the Conservatory. Gently picking up the purple page marker, he placed it between the two pages he'd just read, smiled, and closed the book. He then carried the book back to the shelf and gently slid it back into its original position.

"Well, one down, a bazillion more to go," he said as he stared down the shelf.

CHAPTER 6
Best Cafeteria Ever

There was no way to tell for certain, but Peter thought it must have been several weeks since he'd started this new job of his, and it hadn't gotten any more interesting. It was actually one of the most boring things that he'd ever done in his life. Nonetheless, he did find a way to help get him through it. If he just made his mind go blank, almost become robotic, Peter found he was able to muddle through this painstakingly, agonizingly boring job of turning the pages. But as he stood there, on top of that ladder rung, he could only think about tomorrow, his day off. Those were the days he was now excited about because he could spend all of his time trying to find a way home.

As the evening shadows slipped quietly into the Conservatory, he was turning yet another page in yet another book as the numbness in his fingers stiffened into pain.

"I'm starving," he said as he shook and massaged his hand, hoping to get some feeling back.

Peter looked around the room for a vending machine or snack bar. After munching on nuts and berries for the past several weeks, he was on a mission to find some junk food. When he regained some feeling in his hands, he climbed down the ladder and ran out of the Conservatory.

"A place this big should have an enormous cafeteria," he said, his gaze darting around in a search for sustenance. "Where could it possibly be?"

Up until now, Miss Penntiworth had brought him most of his meals in the morning and at night.

She must have been trying to make this easier for me, he thought, looking around corners and down the halls. *I do like her.*

She reminded him of his grandmother, and that connection to home felt comfortable to Peter. As his stomach sent up a reminding gurgle, his thoughts fixated with food as he tried to remember the last time he bit into a hotdog or ate a hot fudge sundae.

"I give up!" he shouted as he slammed another door shut. "I'll never find it this way."

Frustrated, he thought it would be best to ask someone for directions. The problem, though, was that it was late in the workday, and most of the people were back in their rooms or who knew where by now. The hallways were pretty empty, even on their days off. Other than his occasional spotting of Mr. Grumsby seemingly massaging the walls, it seemed as though everybody here kept to themselves.

Peter was no different. Up until this moment, he spent all of his time busy with the books or exploring forgotten sections of this monstrosity of a building, hoping to find a hidden door that would help him escape. Even if he'd had the time to talk to someone, he wasn't even sure there were any kids around. He had not seen anyone even close to his age. Granted, the place was huge, but he thought he'd at least have found one other kid to hang out with by now. Instead, in order to break up the monotony, he spent most of his free time roaming around and exploring by himself, and yet, after all those hours spent wandering around, he'd never thought to look for the cafeteria.

Where is the end of this place? he wondered as he turned down another empty hall.

He checked a few more doors, but still no cafeteria.

"Maybe it will be easier to just go back and ask someone in my section," he said as he paused for a moment, trying to figure out where he hadn't been yet.

He turned in a different direction, but of course, this didn't matter because any option was as new to him as the last. He never felt as though he knew where he was going or where he had been. Other than the route he took to the Conservatory, Peter couldn't tell one hall from another. Even the people were new. As best he could recall, he hadn't run across the same person more than once since he'd arrived – with the exception of Mr. Grumsby and Miss Penntiworth of course. Most of the people here seemed friendly enough. Each person he'd come across would pass by him and smile. Some would even stop for a moment and say hello. Unfortunately, none of these people were his age, and he was constantly reminded of this when he heard them whisper to each other about how young he was. He didn't like hearing this because it also reminded him of how alone he was, and what little time he'd been given to enjoy life back home.

It all became very annoying. He had nothing in common with any of these people, so he felt like an outcast, just like back home. Without anybody to talk to or to hang out with, it made the time drag on. Miss Penntiworth told him he had to go out and find fun, but he couldn't figure out where to start looking. Peter kept hoping things would change. He kept hoping he would one day find some kids he could spend some time with, but every day he was disappointed.

"I better just find Miss Penntiworth," he said as he walked by the same fountain for the fourth time.

For all of this loneliness and frustration, there was one person, other than Miss Penntiworth, that he was becoming fond of. On his way to his section in the Conservatory, Peter would often pass by an elderly man shuffling down the hall, slower than a snail, just slouched over, minding his own business. He was dressed in pants that stopped just below his chest, and he wore a gray wool ivy cap. He had a walking stick capped with a black billiard ball marked with the number 8. When he saw Peter in the hallways, he'd offer the same greeting each time.

"Hey, Slick. What's shaking?"

Then he'd continue on without another word. One day Peter was particularly frustrated by, well everything, the books, the food, the fact he missed his parents. The little old man came down the hall, and instead of his usual greeting, he said to Peter, "You need anything, ask for ole' Charlie." For some reason, that cheered Peter up. He liked Charlie because he reminded him of the nice old man who owned an ice cream parlor back home. Unlike most of the other people, Peter came across, Charlie didn't look at him with pity or concern. He treated him like he was just one of the crowd, and Peter liked that feeling.

Outside of Charlie, Miss Penntiworth, and being yelled at by Mr. Grumsby, Peter didn't have all that much interaction with other people. Back home, he never really had any close friends, so it wasn't much different here. Today, he ran into Charlie again.

"Hey, Charlie," Peter said with a smile.

"Hey ya Slick," Charlie said, smiling back at him.

He turned around and watched as Charlie continued down the hall. Seeing the old man always put him in a good mood. He turned back around and continued on to Miss Penntiworth's office, and as he turned the corner by Mr. Grumsby's office, he saw her up ahead reading a stack of papers.

"Miss Penntiworth!" he shouted, causing her to jump and drop the papers she'd been reading on to the floor.

"Peter! You startled me!" she said, trying to collect the papers. "How are you?"

"I'm starving!" he said as he scrambled to help her pick up the papers. "I haven't been able to find the cafeteria."

She stopped for a moment and stared at him with wide eyes.

"Oh, my goodness. I'm so sorry, dear," she said as she put the papers under her arm and stood up.

She grabbed Peter by the arm and walked him down the hallway. Peter was struggling to keep up.

"I don't know where my head has been lately. I cannot believe I never showed you the cafeteria. I think I need a vacation. Now, this is important to remember, so please pay attention. Head down this corridor and make the first left. Once you come to the fountain with the inside garden, the cafeteria is the third hallway to the left. Go down this hallway. You will notice a series of sculptures showing men on horses. The door after that is the cafeteria."

Peter just stood there, confused. Miss Penntiworth smiled and took him by the hand.

"Here, come with me," she said.

She led Peter into an atrium. Not stopping to look around, she went past a fountain in the center of the room and down the hall she described until they were at the statues of the horses.

"Here we are. Right inside that door up ahead is the cafeteria," she said, not really paying attention to where she was pointing. "Again, I am so sorry dear. I should have showed you that straight away. Anyhow, I must be off. Please let me know if there is anything else I can do for you dear."

She pulled her papers out from underneath her arm and was again deep in thought as she scurried down the hallway.

Hoping to get the smell of some steaming hot fried chicken, or even better, pizza, Peter quickly scrambled down the hallway. He found a pair of doors but was not sure which one she'd pointed to. Shrugging his shoulders, he opened the first door and entered the room, which looked like many of the others he'd been in. There were long tables with reading lamps on them, and lots of shelves – not as tall as the ones in his section, but tall enough to house what appeared to be thousands of books. As he walked up and down several rows between the bookshelves, he could not find any sort of lunch counter, cook, refrigerator, or plate of food anywhere. It didn't even smell like food in here, just the smell of books. He looked around some more, but compared to every other room in this place, this room was not that large. Actually, it was only about three times the size of Miss Penntiworth's office, so he was certain he hadn't overlooked any nook or cranny. Peter went back into the hallway.

"Well, it can't be this room," he mumbled as he shut the door from the room he was just in. "She was in a hurry. She must have meant this one." he said as he walked across the hall to another door.

As he opened it, he walked in on Mr. Grumsby, who was up to his chin in a steamy bubble bath.

"What in the name of! What are you doing in here?" Mr. Grumsby yelled, burying himself in bubbles.

As funny as the moment was, Peter tried not to laugh as he stared at Mr. Grumsby, who was wearing a shower cap and holding a rubber ducky. Seeing him in this position was almost too much, though, and it took everything in him not to burst out laughing. Nevertheless, he knew he'd made a dreadful mistake, and he would undoubtedly pay for it later.

"I am so sorry, Mr. Grumsby. I was just looking for the cafeteria."

"Does this look like the cafeteria, boy?" Mr. Grumsby yelled as he tried to hide his rubber ducky in a large puff of bubbles. "Well?"

"Well no, of course not," Peter said, awkwardly trying to avoid any eye contact by looking at a lamp.

"Then go across the hall! I figured even you could handle a simple thing like getting dinner for yourself."

"I was across the hall but I couldn't–"

"Do you have to stand there yammering with that door open?" Mr. Grumsby grumbled, cutting him off. "I suppose you would like me to catch my death of cold? Or perhaps have a mob of people parade past me for their amusement?"

Peter just stood there, not knowing what to say.

"In other words, shut the door!" Mr. Grumsby screamed.

"Sorry," Peter said and quickly complied, except he'd shut himself in the room with Mr. Grumsby.

The soapy man looked back at him, astonished.

"Why are you still in here?" he yelled.

"Well, you told me to shut–"

"I didn't invite you to stay, did I?" Mr. Grumsby screamed. His face was a shade of red Peter had never seen before.

"I…I mean, I don't…" Peter stammered.

"Let's see if I can lay it out for you. Go across the hall, pick up a book that you like, and go, have, dinner!" Mr. Grumsby said with a sneer.

Peter scrambled out of the bathroom. He quickly shut the door and went back across the hall. For a brief moment, he was hesitant to open the other door. Even though it was the only other one in that hallway, he was worried it somehow wasn't the right one, and he'd get into even more trouble. After several minutes, he opened the door and went inside. The room still looked the same as before, but this time he pulled one of the books off the shelf and took a closer look. They were different from the LifeBooks that he was now accustomed to seeing. These books looked like the ones that were at his local library. Most of them reminded him of the vacation guides that he and his family would look through. One of the books that he removed from the shelf was titled, *Famous Restaurants of France*. This didn't really appeal to him, so he put it back and looked at a few more titles before taking another book down.

North American Amusement Parks

He liked the way this book looked, and he really loved the idea of going to an amusement park, even though he'd never been to one before. As far as he knew, there was nothing to do but eat, play arcade games, and of course, go on rides, so he walked over to a table, placed the book down, and took a seat on a nearby bench. An enormous roller coaster was displayed on the cover. Peter quickly opened the book and read the table of contents. Each chapter was separated by the location of the park. He slid his finger down the list of states and the parks they hosted and recognized one he'd always bugged his dad about. They were never able to go because his father couldn't get enough time off from work.

"Page ninety-eight," he said as he flipped through the pages.

After all of his time in the Conservatory, Peter could now flip through pages so fast that he created a wind, which blew his scruffy hair back. Without looking, he stopped on page ninety-eight and glanced at the page. Pictures of rides, games, and food of all sorts, including foot-long hotdogs, stared back at him. He started to read the page even though he wasn't sure what to expect or how he was going to eat when he got there, but like everything else lately, it was probably going to be a learn-as-you-go experience.

The mist he was now used to, formed around him, and Peter found himself smack dab in the middle of the theme park. Screams of excitement filled the air, and he ran over to watch people dart in and out of lines to get a second-turn on some ride. With everything happening around him, Peter just stood there, spinning in circles, taking it all in until something caught his attention. Even though there were hundreds of people rushing around, a monster roller coaster whooshing by, and children laughing from the nearby waterslide, the only thing that he focused on was a tiny hotdog stand. It seemed like decades since he'd had one, so he quickly rushed up to the counter and tried to get the attendants attention by clearing his throat. When that didn't work, he waved his arms and shouted, but no matter how hard Peter tried, nothing was working.

The smell of the hotdogs was intoxicating, and he felt himself salivating at the thought of eating a foot-long beauty. He even tried to reach over the counter and grab one, but his hand passed right through. This was frustrating, and he was starving. Not knowing what else to do, he walked over to a nearby picnic table and sat down.

"Why am I here if I can't even eat?" he mumbled. "What am I supposed to do? Is there an instruction manual I missed or something?"

"You have to shut your eyes and ask for one," a girl's voice told him.

Peter nearly jumped out of his skin.

"Who said that?" he asked, frantically looking around.

"Over here," this sweet, soft voice said.

He quickly turned around, and sitting near the hotdog stand was a teenage girl. She was as tall as Peter, had a tan complexion, long dark hair, and was holding a big pink bunny she must have won at one of the carnival games. Peter had never been interested in girls before, but as he looked at her, he felt himself getting nervous and sweaty.

"Sorry to startle you," she said. "I guess you're new. I'm Alexis."

"Uh, yeah, hi. I'm Peter," he said, a little embarrassed to look at her.

"How come you can see me? Nobody else here has been able to," he asked her.

"I'm the same as you," Alexis said. "Dead, that is."

Peter winced. He still hated being referred to like that. Alexis must have noticed how it made him uncomfortable.

"Um, sorry about that," she said. "Anyways, this is one of the fun parts of our lives now. You get to go anywhere you want, when you want," Alexis said as she smiled and looked around. "It's unfortunate it only lasts for a short time, but I guess they don't want us just strolling around the world all the time."

Peter just sat there, staring at her, completely forgetting his hunger.

"I haven't been to this place in a while," she said as she looked at the rides. "This park is really cool. It's got all kinds of… I'm sorry, I forgot, you're hungry."

Peter smiled. He found her interesting. Especially the way she spoke so fast, her words almost meshed into one.

"Look, anytime you want to eat, go to the place that has what you want, close your eyes, put your hands together, and ask for whatever you want. Watch," she said as she pushed Peter over and sat next to him.

Alexis shut her eyes and put her hands together.

"May I have a hotdog, please, with ketchup and a little relish?"

And just like that, it appeared in her hands. Steaming hot, with ketchup and relish.

"Thank you," she said. "See, it's easy. Now you try it."

Peter stared at her for a moment, shrugged his shoulders, held out his hands, and asked for a hotdog with extra ketchup. When nothing happened, he opened his eyes and looked at her.

"No, goofy, you have to put them together like this," she said, helping Peter clasp his hands together, which caused his face to feel like it was on fire. "Try it again."

He closed his eyes and asked again. "May I have a hotdog, please, with extra ketchup?"

In the blink of an eye, it appeared in his hands, and best of all, it was dripping with ketchup.

"Thank you," he said right before he wolfed it down.

Just then, Peter's eyes grew wide.

"Alexis," he whispered, "I don't have any money to pay for this."

She laughed.

"You don't need money."

"But isn't this, like stealing?" he asked.

"No, Peter, watch," she said as she pointed to the vendor.

The man went to throw some trash into a trashcan. On the ground, next to the can, was some cash. The vendor looked around and asked a woman standing nearby if she'd lost any money, but she had not. The vendor then put the money into the cash register.

"It works out where the people find money. I don't know how they do it, but it happens every time," she told Peter.

After finishing her lunch, she stood up and stretched. "It was nice meeting you, Peter."

"Wait. Where are you going?" he asked her. "I want to talk to you. Let's ride a ride or something. I don't ever get to talk to anyone my age."

"Sorry," she said, looking towards the sky. "My time is almost up. Maybe we'll run into each other again. Hang in there. It's not that bad of a place. Give it a chance. Good luck."

As she got up and walked away, Peter watched her evaporate into a mist. He sat there for a moment, his heart as empty as his hands. It felt good talking to Alexis. She was the only person he'd seen even close to his age. He had so much to ask her. Miss Penntiworth was great, but there was no way that she could relate to him.

"Great. Nobody to talk to, and I'm still hungry."

Peter put his hands together and asked for another hotdog.

"I better hurry up and get some more rides in," he said as he gobbled down his meal.

Jumping up, Peter headed straight for the roller coaster.

"This is the one!" he said as he looked up at all the twists and turns the track made.

Other than being the largest one in the park, it also had several upside-down loops, and a bunch of sharp, twisty turns. He noticed an empty car and jumped into it. As he had experienced with people – those still alive, anyway – nobody noticed him. The shoulder braces came down, and the ride began. The car slowly went up the first hill. He beamed with excitement, and his heart raced as he heard the chain clanking underneath him as it pulled the roller coaster up the steep climb. As they reached the top, he looked down on the whole amusement park. He lost his breath and felt goosebumps on his arms as he saw the people below, who now appeared to be no larger than ants.

Suddenly, the roller coaster lunged forward. Peter fell forward like he'd been dropped out of an airplane, and the car plummeted toward the ground until the very last second where it zoomed up another incline. Peter was briefly lifted from his seat, and as the ride continued, he was thrown around and spun upside down. He was screaming so loud he wondered if anyone was able to hear him. The ride ended, and nobody looked at him, so he thought he was safe. As he got off, Peter ran to the back of the line and waited to go on again, before he remembered.

"How stupid can I be?"

He hurried back to the car he'd just gotten out of, nobody noticing him cutting in front of a dozen people. As he waited for the ride to begin, Peter watched the people around him. In the seats ahead, he saw a man rub his son's head in anticipation of the ride. The excitement of the moment began to wear off as Peter remembered his family. Just as the ride was about to begin, a bright beam of light shined down above his head. The next thing he knew, he was back in the cafeteria. After he realized what had happened, he pounded his fist onto the table.

"Man, what a jip. I didn't even get a second turn," he said as he looked around for someone to give him an explanation.

There was nobody there to ask what to do, so he took another look at the book he'd just read. Opening it to the same page, he read the same paragraph over again, but nothing happened. He flipped several pages forward and found an article about another theme park and started to read that. Again, nothing happened. Peter gritted his teeth. His skin heated as he scowled and stormed over to pick out another book from the shelf.

Great Underwater Adventures

I could get fish sticks, he thought.

Within a few pages, Peter found an interesting looking island somewhere off the coast of a place called Belize. According to the article, it was one of the best spots for scuba diving. He started to read about it, but still, nothing happened. No mist, no beach, nothing.

"There must be something wrong," he said.

Standing, Peter took the book of theme parks and hid it on top of a shelf in the corner. This way he'd be sure to find it again. He then ran out of the cafeteria and headed towards Miss Penntiworth's meeting room, walking in just as she was giving instructions to a new group of people.

"So, if all of you can now…why hello, Peter. I trust you enjoyed your meal?" she asked as she took off her glasses and looked at him.

"Yeah, but what the heck?" he asked.

Miss Penntiworth rolled her eyes. "Peter, your language," she scolded.

"Oh, sorry. What I mean is, what happened?" he asked as he walked up to her desk.

"Whatever do you mean, son?"

He explained to her what had happened and how he'd tried to go back, and she laughed.

"Well, Peter, the work has to get done sometime."

"Yeah, but geez, I could have a day of fun and still get my work done. I mean it's not like these books are going anywhere."

Miss Penntiworth excused herself from the class and took Peter out into the hallway.

"Peter, dear, imagine if you could spend your whole day traveling from one adventure to the next. It would be great for you; however, nobody's life would continue down there, because everyone up here would be traveling all over the place," she explained to him. "Therefore, nobody on Earth would be doing anything more than standing there, suspended in animation. In turn, the people who turn the pages, including you, would have nothing to do when they got to the theme park because no rides would be working, no food would be cooked, nothing would be happening."

As if a light had gone off in his head, Peter started to understand.

"In short, Peter, enjoy yourself during your meals, but do so in moderation. There is plenty of time to see plenty of things. However, you are only allowed three visits in a day, and at prescribed times. Each time you enter the cafeteria, you get one turn to go off and eat. You must remember, Peter, that your work here is vitally important. If you and the others do not turn the pages, life does not continue," she told him.

He thought about it for a moment and reluctantly agreed.

"Now if you will excuse me, dear, I have some very confused people waiting for me," she said as she made her way back into the classroom.

Even though he understood the point she'd made, he was still a ten-year-old. Now that he knew how exciting mealtime was, staying focused on his job was going to be that much more difficult. What was once an excruciatingly boring job now got worse. Waiting for mealtime was like waiting for Christmas Day to arrive, and as he begrudgingly returned to his section, he thought about all the great places he could visit. Eating a cheeseburger at a baseball field, chowing down on pizza on top of the Eiffel Tower, sucking on a tube of food on the space station, getting a brain freeze from ice cream on a submarine, the possibilities were endless. He spent the next few hours blindly turning pages and dreaming about where he'd go for his next meal, and when he finally got to the last book in his section, something occurred to him.

"Wait a minute. Maybe this is what I've been looking for!" he said. "Maybe I can use this to get back home."

He thought about it on his walk back to his room. Out of all of the time that he'd spent in this place, going to the cafeteria was the only opportunity Peter had to actually leave, to get far away from the confines of this, whatever it is.

"The next time I go eat, I can just look for a restaurant by my house and go home! I'll have my family back!"

He hadn't been this excited since he met Alexis. As soon as he got to his room, he went to the closet and took out the picture of his parents. The full moon hung outside of his window and illuminated the room enough for him to see their smiling faces. The joy of the cafeteria had now been replaced by the desire to get back home. His head continued to race until he noticed how silent the night was. Back home, he would have heard the clinking of dishes as his parents washed them in the sink or the muffled voices on the television in the living room. These noises gave the darkness some life, and in his room now, there was none of that. It was a stark, cold reminder to him that he was still alone, but now he had a way to change that.

CHAPTER 7
Family

Nights at the Conservatory were the worst for Peter. They were mostly spent lying in the dark, listening for a break in the silence, so he could be reminded that life was still around him. When it came time for breakfast, he hadn't had any sleep, and he didn't feel like moving. However, he was hungry, so he exerted whatever energy he had left to make his way to the cafeteria. Even though he'd thought about it for most of the night, Peter was still unsure how he could use the cafeteria to escape. Just trying to find a book that mentioned a restaurant near his house seemed like it would take an eternity to find. When he walked out of his room, he found the halls deserted, and it was still dark outside. He couldn't remember the last time he had gotten up this early, but he wanted to work on his plan as soon as he could.

"This is going to work," he said, trying to reassure himself.

Since he was new to this cafeteria thing, he thought it would be better to take some time to learn about it before trying to use it to get home. This took some of the pressure off him, and he started to feel a little better.

"I need to find someplace really fun for breakfast," he said with a big smile on his face.

It felt good for Peter to feel excited again. As he expected, there was nobody in the cafeteria when he walked in. Since it was an off day, he assumed most people would take advantage and sleep in. Then again, after turning all of those pages, maybe some people just didn't want to spend the day around books again.

But these are fun books! he thought, smiling as he looked through the shelves.

There were endless amounts of them to choose from, but Peter could not find any that matched his level of excitement. He settled on the book about amusement parks again. He walked over to the far corner of the room and found the book in the same place he'd left it. After he dissipated into the park, he noticed it was still somewhat early, so the crowd was sparse. He quickly found a stand selling breakfast burritos and asked for one, just as Alexis had taught him.

While he sat there eating his breakfast and deciding what ride to ride, something caught his attention. Something that had gone unnoticed by him the last time he was here. The people walking around the park were families. This wasn't anything unusual, but for some reason, he hadn't noticed this until his ride on the roller coaster during his previous visit, and he hadn't thought about it since.

Eating his breakfast burrito alone, he watched as little boys and girls strode by, riding on top of their father's shoulders; mothers were pushing strollers with kids anxious to get out. Suddenly, he didn't feel like going on any rides. He didn't feel like getting cotton candy or winning a big stuffed animal. Peter was alone, with nobody to share all of this fun with. For a place full of excitement and wonder, it had nothing to offer a person who was as alone as he was. The beacon to return him to the Conservatory shined over his head, and he found himself in the same spot he'd started from, holding a half-eaten breakfast burrito.

Back in the cafeteria, his trip to the amusement park had set the mood for the rest of his day. He didn't bother setting the book aside again because he wasn't planning on ever going back to that place. For the next several hours, he moped around the building, but by the time lunchtime came around, he'd started to feel somewhat better, and his appetite was back. This time he was determined to stay away from amusement parks and thought it best to try someplace different. He went to the cafeteria and eventually settled on a book about baseball stadiums. After he opened the book, he found himself sitting in the middle of a huge baseball stadium packed full of people.

"Nice seats," he said as he looked around and found himself along the third base line.

Peter was so close he felt as though he was on the field himself. He could even smell the dust of the infield as the third baseman scooped up a grounder.

"Could I have a slice of pepperoni pizza and a soda, please?" Peter asked as he placed his hands together.

The pizza was warm in his hands, and the soda was chilling his knees as he held it steady. He felt almost alive again, and he spent the next several minutes eating and watching the game. During a timeout on the field, he looked around. Unfortunately, his good mood was once again dashed as he noticed the families in the stands. Fathers and sons laughed and smiled together as they sat dressed alike in the same baseball jerseys and hats. Peter couldn't help himself. His stomach knotted up as he thought about his mother and father.

The crack of a bat caught his attention, and he noticed the batter had just hit a pop fly that was headed right for him. Peter quickly stuck his hand out to catch the ball, only to have it pass right through as though it were nothing more than vapor. A boy about his age rushed over, grabbed the ball, and showed it to his father, who held him in the air and gave him a big hug. Peter was left crying as the light finally shined above his head to take him away from it all.

It was an unfortunate pattern that Peter once again found himself in as he mindlessly walked through the halls of this prison he was in. He didn't know where he was going, nor did he care, and as he passed a grandfather clock, the chiming bells reminded him that it was dinnertime.

"Why bother?" he asked. "Where am I going to end up next, some family reunion?"

He couldn't suffer the idea of having another meal, and he couldn't take another tour of this place either. Deciding to seek refuge, he skulked his way back to his room, making sure he took a way where there was little chance he would run into anybody. After shutting his door and closing the curtains, he lay on his bed, watching the room transform into his old bedroom. For the rest of the night, he just lay there, thinking of the days where he would run downstairs and spend time with his parents. It seemed so long ago, and Peter wished, more than anything, he could have those moments back. He picked up the photo of his parents from his nightstand and stared into their eyes. They seemed so happy when this was taken, but he wondered how happy they were now. Soon enough, he would find out...

CHAPTER 8
A Plan is Born

Light shined through his window as a slight breeze pushed his curtains aside and washed over him. The picture of his parents was still clutched in his hand, which rested upon his chest. He looked at it for a moment, the edges of the picture starting to crumple and fade from him holding onto it as much as he did. He smiled and pressed the picture up against his forehead.

"I miss you guys," he whispered, leaning over and propping his treasured photo up against the lamp on his nightstand.

Taking a moment to swallow his stress, Peter walked over to the window and slid open the curtains. Off in the ocean, he watched the man in the small rowboat cast a line out into the water. Nothing happened for a while, so he got dressed and ventured out to see what was going on today. As he watched all the people in the hallways, he remembered that it was a day to turn pages. Seeing all those families enjoying each other brought Peter to a point where his cares and concerns about getting his pages turned diminished to where it just didn't matter anymore.

"I don't know these people. I don't care about these people. What does it matter to me if they get to their next day?" he grumbled. "All my days are the same; why shouldn't theirs be?"

His mood worsened as he made his way closer to the Conservatory.

"It all turns out the same for everyone in the end. Stuck in this place, with no one around and where nothing matters," he mumbled as he trudged along.

He was tired and bored of this place, and of his so-called afterlife, but it didn't end there. He was also tired of the LifeBooks, he was tired of Mr. Grumsby's attitude, and he was tired of Miss Penntiworth and her attempts to "get through to him." The only thing he wasn't tired of was the fact he could finish his "stupid job" and go to the cafeteria to get away from all of this responsibility and all of these people.

"Maybe one day I can get away from this stinking place permanently," he groaned as he got to his section and trudged up the ladder.

Each page he turned felt heavier than the last, and the mere sight of the next book in line made him nauseous. Nonetheless, he begrudgingly dragged it off the shelf and turned its page. As he looked at the ladder and the rest of the books, he felt himself hating the mere sight of every single one of them.

"If this is so important, why do they have a ten-year-old kid taking care of it? Stupid books. Don't they get it?" he yelled from the top of the ladder. "I hate them!"

Peter didn't bother looking to see if anybody had heard him, or even came over to check on him. It didn't matter.

"I hate the fact that all of these people in these books are living their lives," he groused as he slammed another book back into its place on the shelf. "I hate it that these people have other people around that care about them. They get to go home to their families. Do I have to be reminded of this every single day?"

Peter paused for a moment and took a deep breath. He hadn't felt this angry in a long time, and once he felt better, he took another book off of the shelf. But as soon as he felt that leather binder in his hand, he couldn't slow down his anger, and his heart raced once more.

"They're getting tucked into their beds and read a story!" he said as he flipped the cover open, turned the page, and slapped the cover closed. "Who's tucking me in? Mr. Grumsby? Whatever!"

Peter shoved the book back into its spot, slid down the ladder, and walked over to a nearby window. Taking another deep breath, he stared off into the distance and watched some storm clouds as they headed toward the Conservatory. Flashes of lightning flickered in the distance and were chased by soft rumbles of thunder.

"I hate this place and these stupid books!" he grumbled with his teeth clenched so tightly his jaw ached.

He continued to stare out the window as the rain started to fall. Another rumble of thunder echoed between the mountains that lay motionless off in the distance. He turned around and stared at his shelves with disdain and anger. It was going to take every bit of strength in his body to climb that ladder again.

"This place sucks," he said as he walked over to a table and kicked a chair aside. He plopped down onto the chair and folded his arms. Gritting his teeth, he looked around one more time. There were thousands of books around him, and each one was a person, yet he'd never felt more alone.

"This is going to take forever," he yawned, burying his head into his arms. "I hate it here," he mumbled as he fell asleep.

When Peter woke up, he looked around, thinking he'd been asleep for hours. The sunlight was now shining through the windows, so he assumed the storm must have passed. After several moments of sitting there, trying to avoid the inevitable, he stood up and let out a deep sigh. He pushed his chair back under the table, but when he looked down, he noticed that his parent's photograph was on the floor next to him.

"How did this get out of my room?" he asked, looking around. "Did I bring this with me today?"

He picked the picture up and stared at it for a moment until he started to feel an all too familiar queasiness in his stomach. He frowned and gently slid the picture into his back pocket.

"I gotta get this done," he sighed as he walked over to one of the ladders and pushed it over to another shelf.

But Peter wasn't talking about the books.

"I gotta get out of here," he said as he continued to mindlessly turn the pages.

Distracted by his thoughts, Peter had an idea.

"Maybe I can try my plan when I go to dinner tonight," he said. "Instead of wasting time eating or riding some stupid ride, I can make my way back to my house."

How could that work? he wondered. He still wasn't sure if it could even be done. Then again, if it could work, why hadn't he heard about other people doing it? Even so, he felt it was worth a try.

"Maybe tonight I can find a book about a restaurant near home," he said. "But even if I can't, at least if it works I'll be away from this place for good."

At this point, Peter felt that being stuck next to an erupting volcano would be a step up from his current situation. All of these thoughts got him anxious to get his section done, so he immediately started pulling books off the shelves and turning each of the pages as fast as he could. After he'd finally turned the last page, he closed the book and ran to the cafeteria. He went from shelf to shelf, looking for something that would get him close to home. Remembering a certain place located a short drive from his house, he settled on a dining guide for haunted restaurants. It was an old castle built on a small island. Peter recalled a big fire burning in the fireplace. It made the shadows pop up all around him. He sat so close to his parents that night he might as well been in their laps.

"Maybe it's in this book," he whispered as he looked intently at the table of contents.

As he searched, Peter tried to formulate his plan. "There used to be a little boat that would run back and forth to the island," he whispered as he slowly scanned the pages. He used to always stick his hand in the water as they made their way across the channel. "Maybe I can jump off the boat and dive deep into the water when it's time for me to return. Maybe the light won't find me."

He got more and more excited about his plan.

"Now if I could just remember the name of that place. It started with a 'B', I think it was called Boldt Castle," he finally said.

His father took his mother there for their anniversary every year. When he couldn't find it in the table of contents, he went to the index section.

"There it is!" he said excitedly.

He turned to the page, started to read, and instantly found himself standing in the main dining hall of the castle. It was just as he remembered with long banquet tables lining up in front of two enormous fireplaces. As he looked around, he knew that it would be too convenient to suddenly see his parents there. His luck could never be that good. Nevertheless, Peter went and looked in the other dining areas, but he did not see them. Strangely enough, though, he did run into Charlie, who was wearing a lobster bib and sitting with a family of four in front of a large marble fireplace.

Charlie saw Peter and waved to him.

"Ya gotta try the lobster tail," he told Peter with a mouth full of lobster meat.

It looked good, but Peter didn't have time to eat. Every second was precious to him at this point, so he just smiled and waved to Charlie before heading for the exit. As Peter made his way out the door, he saw the ferry docked at the landing, getting ready to leave. He ran over and leaped onto the boat. His heart was about to jump from his chest.

Everything so far had worked out as planned, and he couldn't be happier. There was a seat open at the front, so he made his way up to it.

Sitting in that seat reminded him of better days. As he looked around, images of his parents appeared before him, smiling with Peter as they all enjoyed a ride in the warm sun, his hand skimming the water. As the boat made its way across the channel, the warmth of the sun was replaced by another beam of light shining directly down on him.

"No! I'm not going back!" he yelled and jumped off the wooden bench and into the water, just as he'd planned.

He shut his eyes as he swam down as hard as he could toward the bottom.

I'm not going back! his thoughts screamed as he reached the bottom of the channel and grabbed on to a rusted old anchor.

There was a tugging at his legs, but that only caused Peter to hold onto the anchor that much tighter. He shut his eyes as hard as he could, hoping if he didn't look at the light, then it would just go away. When the tugging finally stopped, he felt brave enough to open his eyes. He found himself back in the cafeteria, lying on the floor in a puddle of water with his hands grasping a table leg. People were standing around him, just staring. They didn't say anything, but just quietly walked away.

"Yeah, I'm fine. Thanks," he mumbled as he stood up and squeezed water out of his shirt.

There was a slosh as he dropped into a chair and lowered his head onto the table. He was more than frustrated, he was dejected. Charlie showed up shortly after Peter and placed a cooked lobster tail down in front of him.

"Don't get it all over ya," he said as he handed him a lobster bib and left the room.

Peter just sat there for some time, staring at the lobster, trying to figure out what to do.

"I'm not giving up," he said as he stood up and walked back to his room.

CHAPTER 9
Tuna Fish Casserole

As best as Peter could tell, several weeks had passed since his botched escape attempt at the castle. This, of course, meant he'd spent several weeks moping around and several weeks being super angry at anything and everything. However, since he now knew the cafeteria plan wouldn't work, he was now actually able to enjoy his mealtime adventures again. One of the things he'd noticed lately was that when he took the opportunity to leave this place and have a meal far away from here, he actually slept better and felt better. The cafeteria gave him an outlet for all of his stress and anxiety.

He had just reached the halfway point of his section when it finally came time for his break. He dropped everything he was doing and ran to the cafeteria, barely able to control his excitement. Each new day offered him a new adventure, and adventure was something he'd always craved.

"Where should I travel to today?" he said as he reached the cafeteria.

He opened the door just in time to see Charlie.

"Hey there, Charlie."

"Hey there, Slick," Charlie said as he pulled Peter's sleeve to bring him closer. "I got something to tell ya."

Charlie looked around, then bent down to Peter's ear. As soon as Charlie opened his mouth to say something, he stopped and looked around again, which caused Peter to do the same.

Finally, Charlie whispered to Peter, "I found a loophole in the system that none of these know-it-alls picked up on." He stopped and looked around again, then continued. "I always carry two books with me when I go eat."

Peter wasn't sure why Charlie was telling him this.

"It's in case I don't like the food at the place I travel to. If I get someplace and just don't like it, I open the other book and still have a chance to get a good meal before my time is up. A little tip for ya, and I won't even charge ya," he said, rubbing Peter's head.

Peter smiled. "Thanks, Charlie."

"Well, I'm outta here. I got a-hankerin' for some lobster again. If that doesn't work out, I'll try some Tex-Mex." He winked at Peter and tucked the extra book under his arm. "Two books, no worries."

Peter watched as Charlie disappeared from the cafeteria.

"See ya, Slick," he heard him say from the cloud of mist.

Peter waved quickly to Charlie and then went up to the bookshelf and began searching frantically. There was only so much time allowed once you walked into the cafeteria, and he didn't want to waste one second.

"Where to go, where to go?" he whispered quietly as he brushed the spines of books, looking for just the right one. As he walked down a different row, he noticed there was a book hanging halfway off the shelf. He pulled the book out and read the cover.

Retro Diners

He wasn't sure this was the book he wanted to try today, but he was worried he was running out of time.

"Why not?" he said as he opened the book.

One of the pages was folded over, so he reviewed that page. As he read the first paragraph, he found himself in the middle of a run-down diner, which, oddly enough, looked familiar to him. Behind the counter was a chalkboard with the specials for the day scribbled across it in green and yellow chalk. One of the items that stood out to Peter was tuna fish casserole.

"I forgot about that stuff!" he said, smiling as his mouth watered.

This was one of his all-time favorite dishes that his mother used to make, so he quickly ordered it.

"Tuna fish casserole, please," he said as he put his hands together.

Shortly after asking, a plate of tuna fish casserole, with crumbled breadcrumbs on top, was steaming in his hands. He turned around to look for a table, and as he did, he dropped his plate of food, which vanished before it hit the floor. Unable to move, he just stood there staring, trying to catch his breath. He wasn't certain, it seemed like it had been an eternity, but could it be?

He slowly walked over and stood next to one of the tables. A couple was looking at the menu, deciding what they wanted to order. Peter reached out to pull the menu down, and as his hand passed through it, he watched as his mother shivered, and then looked directly at him.

"I just felt a chill, dear, did you?" she asked Peter's father.

"No. Maybe the air conditioning finally kicked in. Would you like my sweater?" he asked her as he felt for his sweater, which was neatly folded next to him.

Peter just stood there, staring at his parents.

"No, thank you. It passed," she said as she stared, pensive for a moment. "It seems so long since we were here."

"I don't know why we always kept coming here," his father said as he took several napkins from the holder and wiped down the table. "This place has always been a dump."

His mother gave a sad smile.

"It's nice, dear. It has a certain atmosphere about it."

"Mom?" he asked.

"Yeah," his father said, sitting there for a moment, recalling his memories. "I think the last time was when Peter was nine. He loved it here. I don't know what it was about this place. The food was never that good, not that a kid would care."

They both sat there, quiet for a moment as they looked down at the table. His mother sniffed away a tear and sat up. She looked so tired and sad. Her once pristine hair was now disheveled; her clothes hung loose. She almost seemed lost. Her stare abandoned her thoughts as she searched the restaurant for something she would never find. Peter felt awful and went over to hug his mother. As he tried, she dropped her glass, which hit the table and splattered water all over, but she didn't seem to notice. She just sat there with an emotionless expression on her face.

"What's the matter?" his father asked, grabbing some more napkins.

"I, I don't know. You're going to think I'm crazy, but I feel as though Peter is here with us," she said, wildly staring all around the room.

His father grabbed her hands and rubbed them reassuringly.

"It's just this place, dear. It's only been three years. Maybe it was too soon to come here. We have too many memories."

"Three years?" Peter said as he almost fell back.

He couldn't believe it had been three years.

"No, no, that's not it. I can't explain it," she said, still looking around as though she was trying to find Peter. "Just to be able to see him one more time, to hold that sweet little face of his and tell him how much I love him, how much I miss–"

Peter looked at her eyes. They were straining for a moment. It was a moment that could not be, for Peter was now being pulled away from the diner and up toward the light. He drifted away, only to catch one last glimpse of his parents. His father was leaning over the table to kiss her forehead. Peter reached forward, toward them, but touched a cold table instead. He was back in the cafeteria. He sat there for a moment with his hand outstretched until he heard a familiar voice next to him.

"Get enough to eat, Slick?"

It was Charlie. He was holding several books and grinning.

Peter didn't answer. He just sat there motionless as Charlie sat down next to him.

"You're too young to have lost your hearing son. What's the trouble?" Charlie asked as he looked over the titles of the books he was holding.

Peter smiled slightly. "I, I just saw my parents."

"How they looking?"

"What?" Peter asked, confused by the question.

"Have they moved on or are they wasting their lives trying to get you back and change what can't be changed and all that?" Charlie asked, somewhat distracted as he tried to figure out where to go eat later.

Peter's forehead crinkled, troubled by Charlie's question. He liked Charlie, but it felt like he was scolding his parents for missing their son.

"I don't know," answered Peter coldly. "I guess they're all right."

"Well, don't get too hung up on it, Slick," Charlie said, now looking at Peter. "The longer you're here, the more chance you'll have of running into someone you know."

Peter was frustrated by all of this. Was it that Charlie didn't hear him? He just saw his parents, not his principal or his dad's barber. Despite his frustration, Peter didn't waste too much time thinking about this. He was stuck on what Charlie had just told him. He might run into his parents again. This gave Peter some hope that he would be able to see them again. This was great because now Peter could just go to restaurants his parents always went to, if he could find the right book, that is.

"How long have you been here?" Peter asked.

"Oh, I don't know. Don't really care, either. Not like I'm in a hurry to get anywhere. Just enjoy where you are while you're there, I always say," Charlie said as he sat there for a moment, then looked around and got up.

"Not a bad place to be if ya gotta be somewhere," he said, staring at the ceiling. "Well, I'll see ya, Slick."

Charlie rubbed Peter's head and walked out the door. Peter took another look at the cover of the book he was holding.

"Retro Diners," he whispered.

He was surprised he hadn't remembered that diner at first. Thinking back, he recalled how he marveled at the stainless-steel siding. It made him feel like he was eating inside of a spaceship. Trying to enjoy the moment he'd just shared with his parents, Peter sat down and reflected fondly of the times that they'd gone there. His father had spent most of the time complaining about the service or the food, but when he looked over to Peter, he'd stop complaining as he watched him sitting with a huge smile on his face, mesmerized by the miniature jukebox sitting on top of the table. Once his father saw how happy he was, he would smile back at him and slide a nickel across the table so Peter could play a song. At the end of the meal, everyone would order large, chocolate malts with whipped cream, and a cherry on top. Of course, his father would give Peter the cherry because he knew how much he loved them. They would then sit in the car on the way back home with stomachaches from eating too much and gulping down the malts too quickly.

"Those were some of the best times," he said, his eyes tearing up.

After looking fondly at the book once more, Peter placed it back on the shelf, making sure he knew where it was so he could find it again. Walking out of the cafeteria, he felt a little melancholy. He cherished this moment but seeing his parents also left him as depressed as when he first arrived. He couldn't get the sight of his mother out of his mind. She was so sad, and he hated seeing her this way.

"I need to get back to them. To tell them that I'm okay, and I miss them."

As soon as he was done turning the pages of his books that night, he ran to the cafeteria for dinner and quickly pulled books off the shelves, determined to find a place where he could go and possibly run into his parents. Peter's head started hurting as he struggled, trying to think of the names of the restaurants he and his parents had gone to together.

"Mom always liked to go shopping. Maybe I need to find a book about mall food courts, or one about that seafood restaurant we used to go to," he said. "No, wait. That place was like a million miles away from home, and we only went there once. Where are the books I need?" he yelled.

As the books piled up around his feet, his frustration turned to panic. He ran over to another section of the cafeteria and jettisoned dozens of books off the shelves even more carelessly than before.

"I'm running out of time," he grumbled through his clenched teeth.

Desperate, Peter hurriedly went back to the diner where he'd seen his parents earlier. Maybe there was a chance they were still there. Rushing past the piles of books he'd left strewn about, he raced to the spot where he'd hidden the book, reached underneath the shelves, and pulled it out. As soon as he found the page that was folded over, he quickly started to read and found himself inside the diner once again. The place was nearly empty.

"Why couldn't they just be here?" he asked as he ran out into the parking lot to look for their car.

It was nowhere to be seen. He slowly walked back into the diner and over to the booth where his parents had been sitting.

"I missed them," he said, slumping down in the seat. He was too depressed to eat, which didn't matter anyway, because just after he sat down, he noticed a bright light reflecting off of the tabletop. Peter looked up and noticed it was time for him to go back. All he could do was stare up toward it and sneer. He knew it wouldn't do any good to try to stay at the diner once the light showed up, and as it dimmed, Peter found himself back in the cafeteria. Several people were picking up the books he'd thrown down earlier. In the mood for a fight, Peter waited for somebody to say something about the mess. No one did. They just turned around and continued to clean up. Peter stood up and walked out of the cafeteria.

"Just because they're letting you off the hook doesn't mean I have to."

That grouchy voice made Peter cringe. Mr. Grumsby grabbed Peter's shirt as he led him down the hall. This was the first time since his arrival that Peter had been back in Mr. Grumsby's office. He hadn't noticed then how meticulous Mr. Grumsby was. Everything was aligned evenly and neatly. From the hundreds of clock and hourglasses to the pens on his desk, everything was precise.

"Now let's get down to work shall we?" Mr. Grumsby walked over to a cabinet and pulled out a feather duster and a rag. "Why don't you start by dusting the timepieces? You might as well become acquainted with them."

Peter scowled, and as he was about to protest, Mr. Grumsby stopped him flat.

"Unless you want to lose your cafeteria privileges of course…"

Peter hesitated and then snatched the duster from his hand. He turned in circles looking at the daunting task before him.

"I'll be over here working. Keep it down so as I am not disturbed." Mr. Grumsby said as he addressed a large pile of documents on his desk. "Replacement, hmph."

Peter spent the next several hours dusting and wiping down all of the pieces. Occasionally Mr. Grumsby would shout out, "Be careful with that!" or "Make sure you put them back properly!" Other than that, the only noise in the room was the shuffling of papers and the ticking of clocks. Peter was surprised that he wasn't as bored as he expected to be. The craftsmanship in the timepieces was unlike anything he had seen before. The smoothly carved wooden arches and the beveled glass gave him a better appreciation for what he thought was a bunch of dusty old antiques. One of them stood out among all the others. Peter walked over to an hourglass majestically situated on a stone pedestal. It was about half the size of Mr. Grumsby and was set on two pivot hinges between two wooden posts. He reached out to pick it up.

"Do not touch that one! You are not ready!"

Peter jumped back. "What do you mean ready? For what?" he asked.

"That is not important." Mr. Grumsby hopped down from his chair. "What is important is that you do as you are instructed," he said as he ever so slightly adjusted the hourglass. "That's enough for today. You know your way out."

Peter didn't know what to say. This day was nothing but one bad encounter after another. He sneered at the back of Mr. Grumsby's head and dropped the duster on the table. As he walked back to his room, he couldn't help but wonder what Mr. Grumsby meant by him not being ready?

CHAPTER 10
The Blue Door

After several hours of lying on his bed tossing and turning, Peter couldn't take it any longer. Everything here was a secret. There was nobody to talk to, and he certainly wasn't having any fun. He had to go home now! He needed his mother, and he missed his father.

"This is ridiculous!" he yelled as he threw his covers off and got out of bed. "I'm tired of this! There's got to be a way for me to get out of here."

Peter stormed out of his room, determined that he would never return, but where was he supposed to go? As he looked down the hall, he saw nothing but darkness. It didn't matter though, he was set on finding that elusive door that would not only lead him out of this place, but away from this place once and for all. Once he was out of the building, he was positive that he could find a way home. It wouldn't matter how long it took to find his parents, he was going to do it. So far, the only thing he knew about the outside was what he'd seen from his bedroom window. There were the woods, and there was the ocean.

"The ocean is no good. I don't have a boat, and besides that, I don't even live near an ocean."

There was a pond near his house, but that wasn't quite the same. That being said, the woods were his only option. So at least for now, he had a plan. He would get outside and make his way through these woods. Maybe then he'd find somebody who could tell him where he was. And then, once he knew that, maybe he could figure out a way to get to his house.

As he went up and down the halls for what seemed like hours of turning doorknobs, he found that most of the doors were either locked - if they were unlocked – the rooms were either offices or they were filled with books. Time was passing quickly, and he was getting nowhere.

"I've got to come up with a better idea," he said as he took a seat by the fountain in the Conservatory, trying to figure it out. "I have to get to those woods, but how?" He sat there thinking for a moment, and then it became clear.

"What the heck is wrong with me?"

If he was going to go through the woods to find his way back home, then why not just climb out of the window in his room?

"How stupid can I be?" he asked as he sprinted back to his room and shut the door behind him.

To make sure nobody thwarted his plans, Peter struggled to push his dresser up against the door. Taking a moment to catch his breath, he ran to the window and pushed it open. The moon was full, and its glow illuminated the trees and ground perfectly, a little too perfectly, however.

"Wow!" he gasped as he looked out the window.

It was only then he realized the ground was a long way down. The best he could estimate, it must have been at least a fifty-foot climb. The outside walls were made of stone, but there didn't appear to be enough space in between the stones for him to grab onto as he climbed down.

Maybe I could use a rope? he thought, but he'd never seen any rope anywhere in his journeys around the building.

Then he recalled a movie he'd watched where a guy in jail tied his sheets together to climb out a window. It had worked in the movie, so that was good enough for Peter. He ran over to his bed, pulled off his comforter and sheets, and laid them out on the floor to get an idea of how long they would be. They barely stretched enough to cover the length of his room, and there was no way that was long enough to get him to the ground.

"Argh!" he yelled, his frustrations getting the best of him. "This isn't getting me anywhere!"

When he couldn't come up with any sort of solution, his frustration turned to anger. Peter walked over to his window and ripped the curtains down to the ground. As the curtain rod hit the floor, he kicked the clump of material away from him. His breathing was fast, and he clenched his fists tight as he looked down at the cloth, and in the illumination of the moonlight, he saw it; the curtains had ripped in half.

His heart raced. "Of course!"

By ripping the sheets, and maybe even the curtains, he could tie them together, make one huge rope, and use that to climb down. With that idea in mind, he got to work. He rushed over to his desk and found a pair of scissors. Stabbing a hole through the sheets, Peter was then able to pull the fabric apart. Once all of the sheets were ripped and tied together, he took one end of the makeshift rope and tied it to the end of the bed. He then took the other end and threw it out the window. Quickly, he stuck his head out to see if it hit the ground. The moon was now hiding behind some clouds, which made it too dark to see, but he wasn't going to let that stop him. Just in case he needed it, Peter struggled to push the bed as far over to the window as he could. This gave him a little extra length on his rope. As he sat on the windowsill, his stomach felt uneasy, and he was getting dizzy.

"Man, this sure looks far," he said as his sweaty palms held tightly on to the rope. "Please don't fall, please don't fall," he kept repeating as he shut his eyes and slowly climbed out.

Once he'd started down the wall, he tried to be careful not to make too much noise when passing by other windows, which fortunately for Peter, were all dark. When he finally got to the end of the rope, the moon was still hidden behind the clouds, making it near impossible to see. The best that Peter could guess, he was still about ten feet too short from reaching the bottom.

"Well, I've come too far now, and there's no way I'm climbing back up this thing," he whispered.

He tried to cram his foot and fingers in between the rocks far enough to get a good grip. It was extremely tight, but it was the only thing he could do to help him finish his climb down. At first, it seemed to be working, so Peter carefully continued his descent down the building, but as he tried to reach for a stone jutting out from a section of wall, Peter slipped and fell. Fortunately, and unbeknownst to Peter, who had not been paying attention, his fall was only about two feet, so he just stood up and laughed.

"Yes!" he shouted, but then clapped his hand over his mouth and looked around.

For all of the obstacles in Peter's way, it was a miracle this had actually worked, and furthermore, he did it without breaking his neck. A thick fog had now rolled in, and Peter could hardly see a thing. In fact, the fog was so thick he could barely see his hand in front of his face. Without knowing where he was going, or being able to see, Peter stood around for a moment trying to figure out if he was doing the right thing. But after everything it had taken to get to this point, Peter was determined to continue on, whether he was scared or not.

In the distance, Peter saw a faint shadow he hoped was the tree line. With no other option, he carefully headed toward the area, hoping he didn't fall into some hole or off a cliff.

It actually felt a little strange being outside again, especially on a night like this where it was eerily quiet. So quiet, he could hear the blades of grass flatten beneath his foot as he took each step. After a minute or so of this, the noise freaked Peter out, so he started to run, but the fog obscured any point of reference. He couldn't tell if he was running in circles or not. It was all too much for him.

Tears ran down his cheeks as he looked for some sign that would give him hope, some indication that he was doing the right thing or at least going in the right direction. Something to tell him everything would be all right, and he would soon be home. Peter found none of that, just emptiness. Scared and lost, he stopped running, hoping to gather his wits about him and to find out where he was.

"Peter?" someone called out in the fog, startling him as he crouched down and looked around.

"Peter?" the voice called again.

He now recognized Miss Penntiworth's voice, but he couldn't tell where it came from, so he decided to run away, determined to not have his plans ruined. No matter how scared or lost he was, there was no way that she was going to take him back to that place; he was going home because this had gone on long enough.

As he continued to run away from her, he couldn't hear his feet hitting the ground any longer.

"Peter?" he heard her ask again.

She now sounded as though she was right next to him, so Peter ran as fast as he could. Nobody was going to stop him from getting home this time.

"Peter, you need to stop," she said softly, her voice circling all around him.

"No!" Peter screamed, barely able to breathe now. "I'm going home."

Peter continued to run, even though he couldn't see anything.

Her voice whispered to Peter again. "Peter, please stop."

After all of his running, she still sounded as though she were right next to him. Peter was out of breath and getting nowhere, so he stopped. Bent over with his hands on his knees, he heard Miss Penntiworth again.

"Where are you going, dear?" she asked in a soft, hush of a voice.

Peter looked up and squinted as he tried to see where her voice was coming from.

"Peter, please talk to me."

The fog cleared and he saw Miss Penntiworth standing a short distance in front of him, but there was no ground underneath her feet! She was floating above a deep canyon, which was illuminated by a thunderstorm just below her feet. Flashes of light exploded beneath her.

Peter looked to his own feet and saw that he too was floating above this canyon! His heart raced as he gulped in a breath of air and stretched his arms out as far as they would go, hoping somehow this would help him stay aloft.

"Peter, dear, it's all right," she told him. "Please come here."

He was too scared to move, so he just shook his head. "No," he said, fixated on the absence of ground below him.

Miss Penntiworth smirked. "Peter, please, it's fine. Trust me." She reached towards him with her hand, but he didn't move.

"Nothing will happen," she reassured him.

Hesitantly, he took a step forward, and cautiously pressed the toe of his shoe onto air that should have been ground. Once his toe rested there for a minute, and nothing catastrophic happened, he moved his other leg to the same spot. When he finally got his feet together, he stood there and slowly looked up at Miss Penntiworth.

"How, how is this happening?" he asked.

"Aren't thunderstorms spectacular?" she asked, watching the flashing of lights scatter below her.

Peter was frozen with fear as she walked over and put her arm around him, only to have him push it away.

"You're not taking me back there," he said to her softly. "I'm going home."

"Peter, I'm not going to make you do anything. You have to make your own decisions."

Gently putting her hand on his back, she nudged him forward. "Just come over here and take a moment to talk to me."

They continued to walk, and after a minute or so, she stopped Peter, stepped in front of him, and lifted his chin gently so she could stare into his eyes. "Peter, you need to do what you feel you must," she told him. "I just wanted to make certain you were all right and knew what you were doing."

"I can't go back there," he said as he tried to choke back some tears.

"Peter, where else are you going to go?" she asked.

He hesitated for a moment and then he told her, "I'm going home."

They both stood there silent until Miss Penntiworth reached out, and tenderly held Peter's face with both of her hands.

"Peter, dear," she whispered, looking closely into his eyes, "you are home."

He didn't know what to say as he stood there staring at her. "What do you mean I'm home?" he finally blurted out. "This isn't home! This will never be home!"

Miss Penntiworth smiled, wiped a tear from Peter's cheek, then stood up and rubbed his shoulders.

"I'm going to go back now, dear," she said as she looked at her watch. "It's almost time for me to retire for the evening. I do hope I will see you later, and if you do decide you want to come back, you will find a path straight ahead that will lead you back to the Conservatory."

Again, she smiled at Peter and walked away.

"I don't want to be here!" he yelled to her.

She just looked up in the air and yelled back to Peter over the rumble of thunder.

"That's all right, dear, I never liked this room much, either."

Peter stood there with his mouth draped open. All of his planning and time he spent only to find out he was still inside!

"This is a room?" Peter said in disbelief. "No freakin' way!"

"Peter, the language."

Miss Penntiworth startled Peter. She had somehow come back to where he was standing and was now directly behind him.

"Sorry, Miss Penntiworth, but how could this be a room?"

She put her arms in the air and turned in a circle.

"Peter, sweetheart, these are all rooms. Remember, size is not relative anymore," she told him.

"Yeah, okay, but why would anyone want to make this a room? There are plenty of things out there that are fun and not so, well, depressing. I don't get it."

"Peter, some people actually find this relaxing. They come here and sit for hours, watching the lightning flash and listening to the thunder rumble and roll as it bounces off the canyon walls. Sometimes you just want to escape, and for some people, this is their escape."

"That's exactly what I'm trying to do," Peter told her. "I want to escape."

He waited for her to respond, but when she didn't, Peter walked up to her and gently held her hand.

"Miss Penntiworth, you like it here, and that's great, but I don't. All I want to do, all I ever wanted to do was to just go home."

She smiled at Peter, let go of his hand, and started to walk back toward the Conservatory. His head dropped, and his shoulders slumped down; he didn't know what to do or where to go from here. It seemed all of his hope was gone, so what next? Miss Penntiworth stopped for a second and stood there quietly. She turned to Peter, walked back to him, and took a deep breath.

"Alright, Peter, if that's what you truly want, I'll tell you what you can do. On the other side of this canyon is a cliff, and beyond that is a door hidden at the entrance of a cave. That door will take you where you want to go," she said.

She then turned away from him towards the path. Peter couldn't believe what he'd just heard.

Is this some sort of trick? he thought to himself.

"No, Peter. It's not a trick," she responded to a question never presented.

"Is that all I have to do? Walk out the door and go home?" he asked, ignoring the fact that Miss Penntiworth had just read his mind.

She stopped, not looking at Peter.

"I didn't say that, dear. That is a door that will lead you out of here. I don't know anything beyond that."

"Well, will I be alive again?" he asked.

"No, Peter. I'm sorry, but you won't be alive again," she told him. "I am not even sure if you can find your way home when you walk out that door. The universe is a very large place. That's all I can tell you. If I could help you more than that, I would certainly do so."

She continued to walk down the path she'd said would take him back to the Conservatory. "I hope to see you again soon, Peter. I do so enjoy your company," she said to him as she disappeared down the path.

Peter turned around and slowly started to walk to the cliff she'd told him about, but then he stopped.

"It can't be this easy," he said, but his heart was now beating with excitement.

Just as he was about to run to the cliff, he realized he was still suspended in air above the canyon, so he carefully stepped forward, seeing the rocks just up ahead.

The thunder rumbled, and the lightning gave him flashes of the rocks he needed to head toward. Once he got to them, he immediately felt better since he was now standing on the ground again. Peter didn't waste any more time wondering if he was doing the right thing; he immediately looked for the cave. There was a formation of rocks near a waterfall, so he walked in that direction. After climbing to the top of the rocks and through the mist of the falls, he saw the cave she'd told him about. It was just below where he was standing, but he'd still have to climb down the jagged rocks and make it over to the other side of the waterfall.

"Well, they certainly don't make it easy," he said as he tried to look for the safest place to climb down.

Running back and forth along a narrow ledge, he spotted a clearing with a gradual drop. Making his way over to it, he sat at the edge of the granite wall and hesitated for a minute before slowly descending. The rocks crumbled and fell as he made his way down to the bottom. Another flash of lightning illuminated the treacherous descent he had before him. There was a series of more jagged rocks ahead that looked like they could cut him into a million pieces, but the worst part was that the cave still appeared to be miles away. There was certainly no easy way for him to get there.

Barely stopping long enough to rest, he took a deep breath and continued down the rocks. At this point, he was exhausted, and it felt as though this night had gone on for days. Now, he found himself on an even narrower ledge, and to get down farther, he would have to extend his leg to a tree branch hanging off the side of the cliff. With no other option, he swung his leg over, his toes scarcely touching the crumbly surface of the rotting tree. As he supported his weight on the branch, it gave way and Peter slid sideways, quickly approaching the edge of the cliff. He desperately grasped another branch as he tumbled forward when another flash of lightning showed him how close he was to falling off the edge.

As he lay there, panting, holding onto that last branch as tight as he could, something dawned on him.

"Why don't I just jump?" he asked. "What's the worse thing that could happen? Miss Penntiworth said I wouldn't be alive again, and I can't be more dead than I already am."

It was the first time Peter had said these words without cringing, and with that being said, he took a deep breath and let go of the branch. It was an exhilarating feeling at first as he slid briefly before rolling over and plummeting headfirst toward the bottom, but as he saw the ground approaching right below him, he panicked and screamed.

"What am I crazy?" he yelled as he fell faster and faster. "Ahhhhh!"

Right before he hit the bottom, Peter closed his eyes. As he crashed into the ground, dust and dirt flew up around him, but he felt nothing. It almost felt like landing on a firm mattress. He wasn't sure what he'd been expecting, other than pain, but there was nothing. He stood up, coughing and wheezing as he looked up to the top of the cliff.

"That was quite a fall," he said, laughing.

Peter dusted himself off and shrugged his shoulders.

"What a letdown. Oh well," he said as he looked around for the cave.

It didn't take long before he saw it just ahead of him, and as Peter pulled away some branches hanging over the side of the cave, a small, bright-blue arched wooden door was revealed. Peter stood there, tilted his head, and looked at the door.

"This is it?"

For a door that was so elusive, and so apparently important, it was somewhat unimpressive.

"Wait, why do I care what the door looks like? It's the door to my freedom!"

After all, his whole goal from the first day he'd stepped foot into the Conservatory was to find a way back home, and here it was, not three feet away from him. But he couldn't open it. He kept replaying what Miss Penntiworth had said to him, or more precisely, didn't say to him. For as smart as she was, and as much as she'd helped Peter since he got there, why couldn't she tell him what would happen if he walked through that door?

Peter dropped down to the dirt and stared at the door, a million questions racing through his head.

"What is waiting for me beyond this door?"

She had told him that he now had to make his own decisions, but there was no guarantee he would walk through this door and end up anywhere near his house.

"Can I find my house? What are Mom and Dad going to say when they see me? How are they going to react?" After all, he'd been gone for at least three years. "Are they even going to recognize me? I would totally freak out if I were them."

Peter stood and dusted himself off. There were so many unanswered questions, but they weren't enough to keep him from reaching for the doorknob and slowly turning it. As he pushed the door open and carefully peeked inside, it was difficult to tell, but it appeared the small door had opened into a large field. Where it was once dark was now awash in brilliant sunlight flooding through the door. He could barely see as he crouched down to enter the doorway, and once he did, his eyes began to adjust to the sunlight.

Looking around, he saw a stone well in the distance, standing all alone and surrounded by nothing but empty field. It seemed oddly out of place. Far beyond that were three dirt paths disappearing into a thick forest. Peter hesitated for a moment so his eyes could adjust to the light, then he started to walk down the hill leading to the well, lost in the possibilities that awaited him.

"Who are you?" a young girl's voice called out, startling Peter.

He hadn't noticed the girl sitting under a tree just a few feet away from him. She was about his age, had brilliant long blonde hair, and held a fluffy golden retriever puppy, curled up asleep in her lap. Peter took a moment to look at her. She looked different than he did. When Peter looked at himself in the mirror, he appeared as he was back home, the same skin color, texture. If you didn't know any different, you'd think Peter was still alive.

But this girl was different. Her skin shimmered, much like rays of sunlight when they bounced off of the rippling water in a lake. With the breeze blowing, her hair moved as though it were in slow motion. It reminded Peter of how his mother's long hair floated behind her when she was in their pool. This girl looked more like what Peter thought a ghost would look like, and he wondered why he didn't look this way. Maybe if he didn't look like a ghost, there was still hope for him to go home and be alive.

"I'm Peter," he said to her.

"Hey. I'm Emily. And this is Jasper."

The puppy lifted his head up and looked at Peter before going back to sleep on Emily's lap.

Somewhat anxious, Peter momentarily stared at the well, but then walked over to Emily and sat down next to her.

"So, what's the story with this place?" Peter asked. "Will it really get me home?"

Emily didn't look at Peter for a moment. She sat there, quietly petting Jasper, but then looked up and nodded her head. Peter's heart raced; he couldn't believe it. Was this it? Was he really going home? *This is too easy*, he thought as he jumped up.

"Well, what do I have to do?" he asked her as his eyes darted back and forth. "I'm ready! Do you know what to do?"

Emily stopped petting Jasper. She had a somber look on her face as she stared at Peter.

"You go over to the well, pick up a stone, and write on it the name of the person who you want to see," she flatly told him as she nodded toward the well. "After that, you throw the stone into the well and pick one of the three paths. The first path takes you to the past, the middle one the present, and the third one takes you to the future."

Staring at the paths, she took a deep breath, then rested her hand on Jasper. Peter had a big smile on his face as he looked back at the well.

"Okay, great! I guess I'm gonna get going," he said as he pointed his thumb to the well. "Thanks for the information, Emily. I really appreciate it."

Emily was petting Jasper again, avoiding eye contact with Peter.

"Good luck," she told him, which caused him to stop.

"Why? Is there anything else I need to know?"

"No," said Emily. "It's all pretty simple."

Peter smiled and again started to walk away.

"But I wouldn't go if I were you," Emily then said.

Peter jerked to a halt, and his smile disappeared. It felt as though somebody had just punched him in the stomach. He spun around and looked at Emily.

"What do you mean?" he asked her. "Why not?"

Emily stared at him and tilted her head to the side as her eyes squinted from the sunlight.

"Are you sad?" she asked Peter.

"Of course I'm sad," Peter said, thinking that was one of the dumbest questions he'd ever been asked. "I want to be with my parents again."

"Well, you don't have any idea what sad is!" Emily said, sternly. "You think you're sad, but you haven't experienced sad until you go down one of those paths."

Peter was confused by what she was saying.

"Why?" he asked. "I thought you said the paths would take me home? How could that be sad? I get to see my parents. I get to go home. That's all I want."

Emily snickered.

"Yeah, you get to see your parents alright," she said. "That's all you get to do."

Peter walked back to Emily and crouched down in front of her. This was getting nowhere.

"What are you talking about?" he asked. "You're making no sense! What do you mean?"

Emily lifted her head and looked into Peter's eyes.

"Have you ever wanted something so bad in your life that you couldn't think of anything else? Have you ever wished for something so much that it hurt just to think about it?"

Peter nodded. "At one time, I thought I did. When I was seven, I really wanted this bike. I thought about it from the time I woke up until the time I went to bed. Every day for a month before my birthday, I asked my parents to get it for me."

"Did you get the bike?" Emily asked.

"Yeah," Peter said.

"Well, imagine if you didn't. Imagine not getting the bike, and then seeing that bike every day and knowing you couldn't have it. Imagine some other kid getting that exact same bike, and you couldn't do anything other than watch him ride it. Day in and day out, the kid rides that bike in front of you, and you cannot touch it or sit on it or ride it. That, Peter, is what you have to look forward to when you go down one of those paths."

Emily looked down at Jasper.

"But that was only a bike. I want this a thousand times more than that bike," Peter said.

"Exactly!" Emily said. "And you know what Peter? This will hurt a thousand times more than not getting that bike."

"Why?" Peter asked. "Won't I get to see my mom and dad?"

Emily glared back at Peter, her eyes blurred as tears formed.

"Oh yeah, you'll see your family," Emily told him as her sadness turned to anger. She stood up and floated over to Peter. "And that's it. You can't talk to them, you can't touch them, you can't even smell your father's aftershave."

Peter stepped backward as Emily came within inches of his face. "What you do get Peter, is a chance to watch them live their lives, and you'll also get to realize what you'll never have again. What's worse yet is that you get to watch them break down crying in front of your grave on your birthday, begging for the chance to change things. You can watch as your parents blame themselves for what happened, unable to tell them that everything is all right. You can also stand there helpless, unable to get your mom to stop crying long enough so she can breathe! That Peter, is what you get when you walk down those paths."

Peter watched Emily as she stared down the paths. She shook her head and then sat back down at the tree. Up until now, he had refused to believe that things could not return to the way they were. That he would be watching his parents like they were on some kind of TV show. He felt sick like he was going to pass out. Bracing himself against the tree, Peter finally slumped down next to Emily.

"I'm sorry, Peter, but you needed to know," she said.

Peter stared at the ground. He then turned to Emily, who looked as sad as his mother had in the diner.

"I had no idea." Peter told her.

She shrugged her shoulders and started to pet Jasper again.

"What can you do? What's done is done," was all she said.

Peter went back to staring at the ground, and then he looked over to the woods. As the wind blew through the trees, Peter watched the leaves float through the air, and then gently settle on the ground.

"What are you going to do?" he asked.

"I don't know. I'm not really sure what I can do," she said.

"Why don't you go back to the Conservatory?" asked Peter.

"I can't. I've moved on from there. The moment I threw the stone into the well, I moved on from there. The Conservatory is not for people like me; it's for people like you."

"I don't know what people like me are," Peter said as he looked at her. "I'm so confused."

"People like you are people who are dead but not really dead," she said, pausing for a moment. "That probably doesn't help you much. Anyways, you eat, sleep, laugh, cry, and do most of the things you did when you were alive. It helps you through your transition. Not me. I gave that up when I tried to go back, so I'm kind of stuck now."

"Are there any other people like you around here?" he asked.

Emily nodded her head to the trees.

"Yeah. The woods are full of them."

This kind of creeped him out, and he backed himself up to the tree as far as he could.

"Don't worry," Emily said. "It's not like we're the ghosts you see in the movies. Nobody goes around saying boo and all that stuff. They're just people like you and me; well, more like me, I guess. We're just kind of in limbo. We're not sure what happens from here, or where we can go for that matter."

"Why don't you hang out with them? You know, the ones in the woods?" he asked.

Emily smiled and looked at Jasper. "I don't know. Jasper and I are pretty happy here by ourselves."

Emily and Peter both continued to sit quietly for some time, just staring at the falling leaves.

"What happened to you guys?" he asked, finally breaking the silence. "I mean, originally."

"Oh, there was a fire," she said. "Jasper ran into the house and tried to save me. He's my best friend," she said, smiling and looking down at her dog.

Jasper lifted his head and looked at her with his tail wagging. They sat there quietly for a little while longer before Emily turned to Peter.

"So, what are you going to do?" she asked.

"I don't know," he said. "I was just asking myself that. I thought things were going to be different. I certainly didn't expect this."

"You can always stay here, Peter," she said. "Go see your parents for as long as you want. Then you can live here, too."

Peter thought about that for a second.

"Would you? I mean if you were able to do it all over again?" he asked, looking at Emily's eyes.

"No," she told him without hesitating. "For as bad as you think it is at the Conservatory, living like this is worse."

Peter just nodded and went back to staring into the woods. He wasn't sure what he was going to do, but this place was as good as any to try figuring it out, and he enjoyed Emily's company.

Peter wasn't sure how long he'd been sitting there, but he finally made the decision to go back to the Conservatory. For as bad as he thought things were back there, he couldn't imagine himself spending the rest of, whenever, sitting here, staring at the trees. Especially since Emily didn't seem happy. At least back at the Conservatory, people seemed content; they seemed to be having fun. Peter couldn't imagine joining them, but apparently, he was the only one feeling that way.

Even though, he still wanted to be back with his parents, but he was pretty sure this wasn't the way to do that. He stood up and wiped the grass off the back of his pants. Emily stopped scratching Jasper and looked up at him.

"You made the right choice," she said to him, smiling.

"I really appreciate everything," he told her, surprised that she knew what direction he'd chosen.

"It wasn't a problem at all," she told him. "It was nice to meet you."

"Is there anything I can do for you or get for you?" Peter asked.

"No, thank you. We've got everything we need," she said as she hugged Jasper, who started to lick her face.

"Well, I'll come back and visit you. Ya know, check on you and Jasper."

Emily gave him a puzzled look.

"I wish you wouldn't," she said.

This surprised Peter.

"Why not?" he asked a little upset at her response. "I thought we were friends now?"

"We are friends, Peter, but put yourself in my place. Every time I would see you, it would remind me of my bad decision."

She then closed her eyes and shook her head.

"Don't get me wrong. I shouldn't say that. I mean, it wasn't a good thing or a bad thing I did; it was just something I was meant to do. But now, to see you, it reminds me of how things used to be. When I was able to laugh and joke, eat a juicy apple, or sleep in on a cold winter's day. So, I have to ask that you stay away once you leave here."

Peter just stood there with his head down.

"I'm sorry, but I hope you understand," she said.

Peter understood exactly what she was talking about, and he felt awful. He wished he could do something to help, and she must have sensed what he was thinking.

"Don't worry, Peter. Jasper and I are fine," she told him. "This is who we are. There's nothing you can do."

"What's going to happen to you?" Peter asked.

Emily put her hands on Jasper's face and looked into his eyes.

"I don't know. Someday we'll figure it out. Until then, we have each other," she said as she kissed Jasper on the head.

Peter smiled at her.

"I hope you find whatever you're looking for Emily."

Emily smiled back at him. "You take care of yourself, Peter. Let go of the past; live this new life of yours. It will make you much happier," she said.

He smiled and nodded. As he slowly turned and walked to the door, he glanced back at Emily, who was still sitting there, hugging Jasper. He didn't blame her for not looking. Peter waved good-bye and opened the door back to the canyon.

Once Peter walked through the door and closed it behind him, he never looked back. He climbed up to the top of the cliff he'd jumped off earlier. The path back to the Conservatory was still there, flashes of lightning illuminating the way. Nothing had changed. When he finally made it back, everything was dark and quiet. Most of the lights were out, and the halls were empty. Exhausted, he walked in and went down the hall leading him to his bedroom. He wasn't sure how long he'd been gone, but since it was dead quiet, he assumed everyone must have still been asleep. As he drew closer to Miss Penntiworth's office, he noticed the door was open, and her light was on.

All he could think about was getting some sleep, but at the sight of her lamplight, he braced for the, "I told you so" conversation he had no doubt was about to take place. Walking quietly past the doorway, he glanced in and saw her sitting on the couch knitting. She never looked up, and Peter thought he'd made it past her without her noticing.

"Have a good-night Peter," was all she said to him.

CHAPTER 11
Gabrielle

As time passed, Peter often thought back to the night he'd met Emily. Things were so different now. He and Miss Penntiworth had hardly spoken since his return. He didn't know what to say to her after all of the trouble he'd caused, and as for Miss Penntiworth, she was too old and too wise to bring up the subject before Peter was ready to talk about it. Even so, he missed talking to her, and now he was looking for any excuse to do so. Since that night, there was something he was curious about, and he thought this was the perfect chance to break the ice. He approached the door of her office and saw her sitting behind her desk, going through some papers, so he softly knocked.

"Good morning, Peter, please come in," she said cheerfully and put her papers down.

Peter walked over and sat on the couch next to her desk.

"Miss Penntiworth, can I ask you something?" he asked.

"Of course Peter. You can always ask me anything. Can I get you a refreshment?" she asked as she stood up and fixed herself a cup of tea.

"Um, no thanks. I was wondering why are there so many doors with so many different things and places behind them? Like that room with that lighting," he asked.

"Well, Peter, we have many people here from many different places in the world, and from different periods in time. Most of them like to go back and see what is happening at a time where they are comfortable. The rooms are nothing more than doorways to the world. We like to make certain that everyone has a chance to go and visit what they remember, or what they like," she told him.

That made sense, but that wasn't what he was really curious about; he was stalling. But since they were now talking, he decided this might be the best time to ask her about that night he'd met Emily.

"When you saw me in the woods that night, what would have happened if I hadn't decided to come back?" he asked.

Miss Penntiworth stood there, staring at the ceiling and stirring her tea as she thought about it before sitting down next to him on the couch.

"I'm not exactly certain, Peter. I cannot recall ever having come across that particular situation," she answered. "However, what I do know is that there are many souls walking around with no purpose or direction. It's a big place out there, and the Earth is but a small sliver of it. Unfortunately, when people do decide to leave the Conservatory, most of them do not find their way back; but the ones that do are warmly welcomed back."

Peter sat there and thought about what she'd said for a moment. Emily was still out there, and he wondered how long she was going to be stuck living by that tree, all alone.

"What happens to the ones that don't come back?" he asked.

"I really don't know, dear," she said with an inquisitive look on her face. "I can only assume that the others become lost for eternity, and unfortunately, a few of them are lost to dark and evil places. But I tend to believe that some find what they are looking for, and then get the chance to move on. Why do you ask?"

Peter didn't want to tell her about Emily, especially since Emily made it clear she didn't want any help. Plus she did ask that Peter stay away. Anyways, she seemed content for the moment to be there alone with Jasper.

"I was just curious is all."

Miss Penntiworth finished her cup of tea without saying much else, but she must have thought Peter had more questions on his mind. "Is there something else bothering you, Peter?" she asked him.

"I don't know," he said. "I guess it's just church and stuff. Everyone always tells you that Heaven will be full of fun and happiness, but all I do is wake up, go to a job I couldn't care less about, and take books on and off shelves all day. I would've thought I'd be having fun, but what kind of fun is this? There's no one around here my age, and nobody really talks to me, so where is all of this fun I've been hearing about?"

Miss Penntiworth smiled at him.

"Peter, Heaven is many things to many people, and it is up to each person to find out who they are and what makes them truly happy," she said to him. "Now, understandably, you have been unhappy since you've arrived, but you also have been unwilling to accept what has happened. Therefore, instead of embracing this new life, you have fought against it and tried to escape it. You have left your happiness behind, and the one thing you must remember, Peter, is that happiness will not find you; you must go out and find it."

Peter sat there for a moment, trying to figure out how he was supposed to find happiness. Where he thought happiness was would apparently only lead him to more sadness. At least, that was what Emily had told him. So, for the moment, Peter left the issue alone.

"Well, thanks," he said as he stood up and made his way over to the door.

"Peter, if you have any more questions or concerns, please come talk to me. You know I am always here for you."

The talk with Miss Penntiworth and Emily caused Peter to rethink his situation. Instead of just blindly turning the pages in his section, he would actually take the time to read about some of these people, to take part in their lives. Miss Penntiworth told Peter when he'd first arrived to the Conservatory that a part of everyone's journey in life was to touch the lives of many others. So now, when he went to work, he was not just content turning the pages of the books. Within each volume, he spent time looking for ones of exciting people. Not only would this get him more involved in his job, and possibly achieve one of life's assignments, he might actually start to have fun.

So today, as with every other day, Peter climbed the tall ladder and took his first book off the shelf. But unlike every other day, Peter didn't just blindly turn the page once he'd opened this book; he actually read it. It didn't stop with the first book either; Peter continued to read each and every book in his section. As the day continued, Peter discovered more and more interesting people. Some were astronauts, some were racecar drivers, and there were even several who played major league baseball.

It was great that Peter had a newfound interest in his job, but the problem was that he didn't know how to balance his time. Although Miss Penntiworth was happy to see him looking for fun, she also realized he was spending too much time reading the LifeBooks. The day would not be complete until all of the pages in all of the books, on all of the shelves, had been turned and he was holding everybody else up in the Conservatory.

Before the next workday, Peter stopped by Miss Penntiworth's office, and sitting on the table next to her desk was a plate of warm chocolate chip cookies. What was once a favorite food was now a signal that he was going to be getting a lecture.

"Good morning, dear. I just wanted to thank you, and let you know that you have been doing an amazing job lately, so I thought I would treat you to some delicious cookies," she said as she sat on the couch and smiled.

"What did I screw up now?" Peter asked.

Miss Penntiworth just frowned at him. "Well, first of all, I think we need to work on your language," she scolded as she placed a cold glass of milk next to him on the table. "As for what you did wrong, I would have to say nothing. Sort of."

He knew where this was going, so he slumped down onto the couch and grabbed a cookie.

"Peter, honestly, you are doing an amazing job," she told him as she handed him a linen napkin. "You have really started to get involved with the people in the LifeBooks, but you also have to remember that life needs to continue to move forward."

"What did I do?" he asked.

"Nothing, dear. You just have to try to keep things moving along," she explained to him. "Have you ever had a day where you thought it would never end? It just seemed to drag on and on?" she asked.

Every day that I've been here, he thought, but instead of answering her, he just nodded. He didn't feel like getting in trouble for mouthing off again.

"That is what you are causing when you dawdle and do not turn the pages," she told him. "I'm not saying that you shouldn't take the time to read the pages of the LifeBooks. It's good that you have an interest in other people's lives other than your own. What I am trying to tell you Peter, is that even though you take the time to read a page or two, make certain you finish what you need to finish."

Peter just sat there, looking at his feet. It was an all too familiar feeling. He felt lately as though he was getting lectured every day. All he wanted to do now was get out of her office as fast as he could. As all of this ran through his head, he remembered that she was talking to him, so he looked up at her quickly.

"It's not fair to everyone else if their lives are on hold because you are bouncing around from book to book looking for excitement. You know this building itself is full of excitement and adventure as well."

Peter was now looking at her and nodding his head.

"The next time you finish your duties, well, hopefully, finish them on schedule anyway, take the time to explore the building. There are great and wonderful things that take place outside of the confines of the bookshelves. Do you understand, Peter?" she asked.

Peter nodded his head and smiled. "I'm sorry. I'll try to do better," he told her.

"I know you will, dear," she said.

Peter left her office in a somewhat foul mood. "What do they want from me?" he asked. "First, I'm not doing enough. Now, I'm doing too much. I can't win."

His mood continued to be sour as he made his way to his section. He kicked a chair aside and sat in it. As he spent the next several minutes looking at the shelves in his section, he thought back to Emily.

"Maybe it wouldn't have been such a bad thing to live like Emily. At least I would never have to see these stupid books again or get lectured all the time."

As he sat there feeling sorry for himself, an annoying sound caught his attention. It was one of the helpers pushing a cart full of LifeBooks. Each day, that same annoying, squeaky cart would wheel in new books to his section and take away old, finished books. When he first started working in the Conservatory, he used to cringe upon hearing this sound. That high-pitched squeak meant there were more books to tend to. Over time, he hardly noticed the noise any longer, until today.

"Ugh. It's going to take everything in me to climb up that stupid ladder."

As he sat there grousing about his job, his thoughts focused on quickly finishing his section so that he could get out of there. The helper finished putting all of the new books in his section, and as she pushed the cart out, Peter listened while the annoying squeak of the cart disappeared among the shelves. He slowly stood up, and just as he'd started turning the pages again, one of the new books on the uppermost shelf caught his eye. Reaching for it, he took it in his hand and was amazed how thin it was. It could hardly be called a book, for it was no more than ten pages thick. Peter opened it and started to read.

"Thomas and Carol had been trying for seven years to have a baby. Today, their first child is born. It is a little girl, and her name is Gabrielle."

Peter was now in the hospital room watching Thomas kiss Carol as she rocked baby Gabrielle and softly kissed her on the forehead.

"Gabrielle doesn't know where she is or who these people are, but she feels strangely comforted," the book read.

As Peter watched Thomas and Carol, he noticed a doctor walk into the room, closely followed by a nurse, who was pushing a strange crib in front of her. As the doctor talked to Thomas and Carol, Peter saw the nurse take Gabrielle, and place her into the crib.

The voice above continued to narrate.

"Gabrielle is being taken away from the comfort of her mother and father; she is scared and starts to cry."

Peter wasn't sure what to make of this, but he could feel Gabrielle's fear.

For most of his time in the Conservatory, Peter never knew what time it was, let alone what day it was. There were no calendars, and few clocks other than the ones in the offices, but over the next several days, he was suddenly aware of every minute as he watched the page marker in Gabrielle's LifeBook get closer and closer to the end. Each day, he took the time to read her book, and he learned that Gabrielle had a rare disease and her body was slowly shutting down.

"Her parents only got to hold her one time," Peter whispered as he held Gabrielle's book.

Thomas and Carol spent every day with her, but the only way they were able to embrace her was by holding her hand through plastic gloves attached to the enclosed crib. Gabrielle had tubes running in and out of her, and she didn't look as comfortable as she had when Peter first saw her.

He knew this little girl would be gone soon, and he felt ashamed. He thought about the times he'd gone on and on about how he was too young to die, that this never should have happened to him. How unfair life was since he was not given the chance to live it. This thin little book changed all of that. This book made him realize how lucky he'd been. If nothing else, at least he'd had the time to experience a family, to swim in the ocean, to play games outside, even to hear the simple little things like a dog bark or a bird chirp. This little girl, represented by this thin book, would experience none of that. She'd never go trick-or-treating, she'd never wait anxiously for Christmas, nor would she ever feel a warm summer wind. She would spend her short life in this sterile environment, never to be touched or feel the warmth of a loving embrace again.

As the pages neared the end, Peter couldn't bring himself to read any longer. Every time he turned the pages, he could only imagine Gabrielle still in the hospital. Maybe they were doing surgery on her, or maybe there was some new medication they were trying. The only problem was that it gave Thomas and Carol false hope. Peter knew differently. He knew nothing they tried was going to work because there were only so many pages left in Gabrielle's book. Peter struggled with the book each day; whether he was turning the pages or thinking about it in his room, Gabrielle never left his thoughts.

It was the last day to turn little Gabrielle's pages. Peter wanted to read about it, to experience what she and her parents were going through, but he couldn't bring himself to do it. All he could do was give the book a gentle squeeze, hoping Gabrielle would feel it and get some sort of comfort. He turned the last page and laid it on its side. There it would lie until another library helper came along and placed Gabrielle into her purple cover.

Peter pulled up a chair and sat next to the shelf that held Gabrielle's book. He must have stared at that little book for an hour before finally getting up and walking away from his section. Later that night, as he was sitting alone in his room, he gave thanks for the opportunity to enjoy the life he had been given. He spent the rest of the night feeling sorry for this child he'd never known, and he wondered what Gabrielle's family was doing right now. It was incredible how such a small book, in such a large library, could easily be forgotten about and overlooked because of its' size. How such a small book could mean so much to somebody and have such an impact, even from such a short existence.

"No more," Peter said, looking up at the ceiling.

CHAPTER 12
The Tattered Tapestry

Peter's nights used to be filled with thoughts about his family and how he was going to get home. Now, he stayed awake, thinking about Gabrielle and her family. After seeing how short life could be, he now appreciated the time he'd spent with his family and was becoming more accepting of where he was now.

That morning, Peter wasn't hungry, so he thought he'd go right to his section. While at work, he still took his time reading excerpts from most of the LifeBooks, which of course caused him to lag behind and have to stay late in order to get everybody in his section to their next day. Today wasn't any different. He didn't know what he was looking for, but he wanted to find something to help take his mind off of Gabrielle.

It had been quite some time since the sun had set that day. The evening shadows had begun their silent journey across the marble floor when a thud echoed from the corner of the room, causing Peter to jump. The nerves on the back of his neck tingled as he slowly climbed down the ladder and peeked out from behind a shelf. There was no sound, and the only movement was from shadows dancing off the walls as the candle flames flickered.

"Hello! Is anyone there?" he called out.

Peter heard a door squeak and then close. Taking a gulp of air, he cautiously headed to the direction of the noise. As he reached a concealed corner of the room, he noticed an old, faded tapestry. Peter didn't come to this part of his section often, so he didn't recognize the cloth. It had very little color left to it, and the edges were tattered, but there were still two discernible figures woven into the fabric. A man and a woman stood holding hands in front of a tree. One side of the tapestry was stuck between the wall and a door, apparently from someone who hurried through without ensuring it remained hidden. Peter's hand shook as he opened the door and peered inside. Just beyond the entrance was a darkened staircase curving downward, but he could not see beyond the first couple of steps.

"Hello!" he called out, only to hear his own voice echo down into the darkness.

He slowly stepped down onto the first step. The room was much colder than in the Conservatory. He shivered as he stepped onto the second step, and as he did, he thought he heard a faint hissing noise in the distance. Not feeling too adventurous at that moment, Peter backed his way up the stairs, shut the door, and went back to his section.

"I wonder if Miss Penntiworth knows what's down here?" he said as he stared at the tapestry.

After he'd pushed the library ladder back to the beginning of his section, he ran over to Miss Penntiworth's office to find her sitting down reading a newspaper.

"What some people won't do to get ahead," he heard her say.

"Excuse me, Miss Penntiworth," he said, knocking on her door.

"Well, Peter, how nice of you to visit with me," she said, setting her newspaper down. "To what do I owe this honor?"

"Miss Penntiworth, where do the stairs behind the tapestry go?" he asked her.

"What stairs are you referring to, Peter?" she asked.

"They're behind the tapestry, in aisle 23, I think," Peter explained to her.

Miss Penntiworth looked at him inquisitively.

"I cannot recall that tapestry, Peter. Could you describe it for me?"

He thought for a moment. "Well, it has a man and a woman standing next to each other, and they're holding hands in front of a tree. I think another person was looking at them from behind the tree."

"I know exactly what tapestry you are describing, dear, but there are no stairs behind it."

Peter hesitated, thinking he'd described the wrong tapestry to her, or maybe he'd told her it was in the wrong section.

"No, I'm sure I'm right. There are stairs there, I saw them," he said. "I walked over and pulled the tapestry out of the door. When I pulled the door open all the way, I saw stairs going down, but it was too dark to see where they went."

Miss Penntiworth's eyes widened. "Maybe you should show me this door, Peter," she said as she dropped the newspaper to the ground and stood up.

"Sure, come this way."

Miss Penntiworth grabbed his shoulder. "Wait just a moment, Peter. First let me get Mr. Grumsby."

"Do we have to get him?" he asked.

"Why, Peter, is there a problem?"

"He makes me uncomfortable. I don't think he likes me too much."

"Oh nonsense, Peter. Wait here, I'll be right back."

Peter just stood there, staring at the door in Miss Penntiworth's office.

Why would anybody be afraid of a door? he thought as he rocked his feet back and forth.

She returned a short time later with Mr. Grumsby scurrying behind her, his little legs struggling to keep up. Peter had never appreciated how short Mr. Grumsby was until he saw him standing next to her. Now he watched in amusement as this man, half the size of Miss Penntiworth, scurried along. Noticing that Mr. Grumsby's visor was curved upward, Peter knew something was definitely wrong. In his hand, he carried the dusty hourglass Peter wasn't allowed to touch. He didn't pay any attention to Peter as he walked past him.

"All right, Peter. Lead the way," Miss Penntiworth said.

Peter took them to the area of aisle 23, where hidden around a dimly lit corner was the tapestry he told her about. The three of them slowly walked up to it, and as Peter reached forward to pull it aside, Mr. Grumsby grabbed his arm and stopped him.

"Step aside, boy," he grumbled as he pushed Peter's arm away, and cast him aside. He then shoved the hourglass into Peter's chest and scowled. "Listen boy and listen good," he said. "If there is a door here, you better make certain you're ready to tilt this hourglass on its side."

Peter looked at the hourglass. It was roughly two feet tall and obviously old, but he couldn't understand why Mr. Grumsby wanted him to do this.

Mr. Grumsby turned to the tapestry, and then stopped for a moment as he put his hand behind his ear, almost like he was listening for something. Peter wondered what Mr. Grumsby could possibly be listening for; it was just a door.

Mr. Grumsby turned to Peter again. "Remember, boy, if there is a door here, you tip this hourglass on its side so that the sand does not flow from one bulb into the next. Do you understand me?"

"Yes, but why?" Peter asked.

Mr. Grumsby, his visor now dipped low over his eyes, gave him a look, which Peter took to mean that he ought to listen and not speak. He got the feeling that Mr. Grumsby didn't like explaining himself to anyone, let alone Peter, so he just looked up at the ceiling and sighed.

"Right, tip the hourglass to the side, no sand, got it," he repeated to Mr. Grumsby, who scowled at Peter's sarcasm before turning back to the tapestry.

With his hand noticeably trembling, he cautiously pulled it back, but there was nothing there except for a solid-stone wall.

"I know it was there!" Peter yelled as he tried to explain himself. "I saw it just ten minutes ago. I'm not crazy."

Mr. Grumsby put his ear up against the wall, almost as though he was expecting the wall to tell him a secret.

"I'm sure there was a door there," Peter plead to them. "I saw it; I opened it. How could a door–"

"Quiet, boy!" Mr. Grumsby snapped as he abruptly cut Peter off.

Mr. Grumsby turned to Miss Penntiworth.

"Miss Penntiworth, would you come over here?" he asked.

She put her hand on Peter's shoulder and gave it a gentle squeeze as she walked past him and up to the wall.

"Put your hand here," Mr. Grumsby told her.

He pointed to a seemingly insignificant stone on the wall. She placed her hand on the spot where Mr. Grumsby's hand had been, keeping it there for a minute before removing it. She then put her hand in several more locations before turning to Mr. Grumsby.

"I cannot tell. Perhaps," she said.

"You think the boy is being targeted?" Mr. Grumsby whispered.

Miss Penntiworth looked at Peter, who was straining to hear what they were saying.

"No, impossible, not Peter," she answered softly.

"Hmph," Mr. Grumsby said as he leered at Peter.

After several more uneventful minutes, Mr. Grumsby placed the tapestry back in its original position. He then turned to Peter and gave him a stern look.

"Boy, stay away from here."

Without another word of explanation, he grabbed the hourglass back and scurried out of the room. "I'll forward the information, Miss Penntiworth," Mr. Grumsby called back as he hurried down the hall.

Miss Penntiworth turned to Peter. "Peter, perhaps it is best that you stay away from this area," she told him.

"What's the problem?" he asked her.

"Oh, nothing to worry about, dear," she reassured him. "Just a precaution is all."

Miss Penntiworth put her arm around Peter and led him away from the tapestry. Even though he was just told not to, he looked back, now fixated with that portion of the wall. Miss Penntiworth put her index finger underneath Peter's chin and redirected his all too inquisitive stare. As they walked away from the tapestry, he had a million questions racing through his head. He settled on the one about the hourglass that Mr. Grumsby had been carrying.

"Miss Penntiworth, why did Mr. Grumsby show up with that hourglass?" he asked.

Miss Penntiworth hesitated for a moment and then smiled. "Let's have a seat over here, Peter." They sat on a wooden bench. "That hourglass Peter is an ancient timepiece created long before any of us were around. It is extremely rare and special. Actually, it's one of a kind. The wood it's made from is called Cupressus sempervirens."

"Super what?" Peter asked.

Miss Penntiworth laughed.

"Some people call it gopher wood. That is the same wood Noah used to build his ark. The sand inside the bulbs of the hourglass comes from the deserts of Jericho, and the whole piece rests on a stone dug up from the region of Mount Sinai. It is believed that the stone is from the remnants of the boulder the Ten Commandments were created from. Legend has it that angels crafted the hourglass as a gift to God Himself."

Peter stood there, his mouth gaping open. He couldn't believe what he was hearing.

"It is also said that God places this special gift in the hands of one of His faithful servants," she told him. "Believe it or not, Peter, that hourglass controls time itself. As long as the sands in that hourglass flow through its bulbs, life moves forward. Once the sand stands still, so does time…and life. If someone were to destroy that hourglass, they would destroy all life as you and I know it."

Miss Penntiworth stood up and walked up to the wall she'd checked earlier. She placed her hand on the surface and stared at it.

"There are certain forces, Peter, that seek this hourglass," she warned. "So the person in control of that hourglass has an enormous responsibility. They must make certain that the hourglass is never lost or stolen and that time moves on. They must do everything within their power to protect it."

"Mr. Grumsby told me to pivot the glass to its side if anything happened. Why did he want me to do that?" Peter asked.

Miss Penntiworth took her hand off the wall and walked back to Peter.

"You see, Peter," she said, putting her hand on his shoulder. "If anything had happened to cause us great harm or danger, you could have frozen time so we could figure a way out of that problem."

"Well, wouldn't we have been frozen, too, unable to move or do anything for ourselves to get out of trouble?"

"We would have, yes. However, Mr. Grumsby has a special gift. He is one of the few who are allowed to move when others cannot. The person who is entrusted with the hourglass is given that power. This power is also given to the one that is in possession of the hourglass as well. If something had happened back there, everyone would have frozen along with time. However, both you and Mr. Grumsby would have had free movement and could have helped us out of the situation. That hourglass is never out of Mr. Grumsby's sight. Now, why don't you head off to bed, dear? You've had a long day."

After all that, Peter wasn't tired, but he knew he'd better listen.

"All right, Miss Penntiworth," he said. "I'll see you tomorrow."

"Enjoy your day off," she told him.

It was all Peter could do that night to get any sleep. All this talk about magical doors and hourglasses had left Peter's mind racing. By the time morning came around, Peter felt as though he'd only just gone to bed.

"Ugh, I'm exhausted," he moaned as he rolled over and stared at the sunlight filtering through the trees.

At this point, trying to get any sleep was useless, so Peter got out of bed and got dressed. He spent most of his day doing his usual walking around and exploring, but the tapestry still intrigued him. Even at mealtime, he would sit wherever, eating whatever, and all he did was think about the tapestry. Throughout the day, Peter kept sneaking into his section to see if the door had reappeared, but much to his dismay, it had not. He was now beginning to doubt that he'd even seen it in the first place. Fortunately for him, by the time he got to bed that night, he was too tired to think about it any longer.

CHAPTER 13
Bobby

Several days passed, and Peter gave up on the tapestry, returning his focus to completing his job. Darkness had fallen outside when Peter finally finished his section. This part of the day was the most difficult, because he was usually alone, always being the last one to finish up. The room was faintly illuminated with only the flickering candlelight from the chandeliers. Peter closed the last book in his section and stretched his arms into the air.

"I can finally put this thing away," he said as he slid the library ladder over to the beginning of his section, the wheels squeaking as they rolled across the ancient grooves worn into the marble floor.

As he walked towards the large doors, Peter noticed a shadow on the floor that appeared oddly out of place. Even though he couldn't make out what was lying there, Peter instinctively looked to the tapestry.

"What..." Peter's words escaped him as his breath disappeared from his lungs.

The tapestry was pulled to the side, and the mysterious door had reappeared. He turned his attention back to the shadowy object on the floor. Now he was scared, and every noise he heard made him jittery. Everything in the library normally felt spookier at night when no one else was in there, and the door's return didn't help. The room was so silent now. Peter could almost hear the heartbeats of the persons that the books represented. As he inched his way closer to the shadow, he kept a vigilant eye on his surroundings. Every creak, every thud, got a reaction from him. When he was within arm's length to the shadow, he saw it was just a book. Peter stood there, shaking his head.

"I work around these things all day, and now I'm afraid of them?" he whispered as he smiled and picked the book up off the floor. "That's odd, though." He paused. "I don't remember this being here earlier."

Peter looked at the cover, hoping to recognize the name so he might have some sort of idea where the book belonged. As he read the title, Peter's eyes widened and filled with tears. His whole body trembled, yet he couldn't move. It wasn't until he'd dropped the book on the floor that he was able to back away from it; as it hit the floor with an echoing thud, the golden letters embossed onto the cover shined in Peter's eyes.

Robert Crones

"Bobby," Peter whispered as he fell back onto the floor.

Peter just sat on the floor, in shock, barely able to feel how hard and cold the marble was. The book still lay on the ground where he'd dropped it. The surrounding candles made the shadow from Bobby's book flicker across the floor, taunting the bottom of Peter's feet. His mind raced as he tried to figure out how this book ended up in his section.

"Maybe it dropped off one of the carts," Peter whispered, looking around for a purple sheath.

He then looked back to the book. The page marker is in the center of the book, so it was definitely not a new book.

The door was now but a distant memory as Peter walked up and down his section, looking to see if there was an empty spot on any of the shelves. Maybe it had somehow fallen from the shelf, but there was no open spot that he could see. Plus, he didn't remember the book being in his section.

"This can't be right," he mumbled. "I would certainly have remembered that Bobby's LifeBook was in my section if I'd seen it before. Maybe somebody put it here on purpose. But if so, why would they do that?" he asked.

Peter thought back, but he didn't recall hearing anybody enter the corridor while he was there, and anyways, nobody really knew what role Bobby played in Peter's life. If somebody did know about it, then maybe they were trying to help him find some answers.

"Maybe somewhere in this book, I can find out why I never had any friends, or why I wasn't popular," Peter surmised as he tried to make some sense of all of this. "Maybe inside this book, I can find out why Bobby hated me so much, and why Bobby got me killed!"

As all of these questions raced through Peter's head, he paced back and forth in front of the book. He never took his eyes off of it, even being so brazen as to walk up to it and tap the spine with his foot, waiting for a signal or some sign of life to make itself known. Peter then bent over and cautiously picked it up, not knowing what, if anything, to expect. But as Peter held it, all he could feel was his hatred for Bobby flowing through his head, to his arm, and finally to the fingertips holding that book, Bobby's book.

The years of torment, the countless times Bobby had thrown rocks at Peter, the times he'd pushed him up against his locker, made fun of him, tripped him, all of these memories came to life as Peter stood there holding that book. He'd never thought he could feel so much anger toward anything, let alone a book; he never felt so much hatred to anyone or anything as he felt now. This book, this person, was the cause of his sorrow, of his loneliness. This book had taken Peter away from all he knew, all he cared about. This book was the cause of his parent's grief and distraught.

As the image of Peter's mom sitting in the diner came to his mind, all he could do was stare at the book. He couldn't help the disgust and anger he felt. These emotions surged through him; they began to consume and control him. Peter glowered at the book until he flipped it open and read the page glaring back at him.

As Peter read the words, he found himself standing in a bathroom he didn't recognize. It was as dark and empty as the library, but Peter wasn't the only one there. He looked over and saw Bobby standing in front of a medicine cabinet, fixated on his reflection in the mirror. The fluorescent bulb above his head flickered in the background, trying to stretch out its life a little longer. Bobby was older than Peter remembered, and as he stood there, he watched Bobby stare into his own lifeless eyes, cold and deep in his head. Bobby never took his eyes off himself as he picked up one of his father's beers he'd placed in the bathroom sink. He pulled back on the tab, and the hiss from the can echoed through the silence. He placed it on the edge of the sink. His eyes never moved away from the mirror, and as he stared at his reflection, Bobby picked up a bottle of his mother's sleeping pills. Pills that had given her the only peacefulness she'd known in twenty years of marriage. Bobby poured the pills into his hand and counted them.

"Fifteen," he whispered. He threw his head back as he filled his mouth with the pills. "That's how old Peter would have been now."

Staring into the mirror once again, Bobby picked up the beer, and without any hesitation, put it up to his mouth and began to swallow the cold, golden liquid. The bitterness of the beer slid down his throat, taking the pills with it. He was disgusted that this swill he tasted was the one thing his father cared about. It was the thing his father loved even more than his own family. This disgusting liquid was what kept Bobby from having a happy, normal family life.

Bobby finished the last bit of beer and threw the empty can against the wall. Then he picked up a picture resting in the sink next to the other cans he'd collected there. He backed up slowly, staring at the picture until he was stopped by the cold, dirty tiles on the wall. Peter watched as Bobby's back slid down the wall until he ended up resting on the floor of the bathroom. He propped himself up and continued staring at the picture. Peter walked over and took a look. It was a class photo, and there, standing in the third row, was Peter, staring and smiling, which was something Bobby wished he could do.

"How could I have been so mean?" Bobby asked. "What did this kid ever do to me?"

These were the questions that Bobby had asked himself a hundred times every day since Peter's death. He was broken, but there were no more tears to shed. As he looked at himself standing two rows behind Peter, he wasn't smiling in the photograph. Bobby couldn't remember the last time he'd smiled or laughed. His eyes seared a hole into the image.

"I'm getting off easy," he said out loud.

His stomach cramped a little, and he began to feel drowsy. Bobby set the picture on the edge of the toilet. He continued to stare at it until his eyelids slowly closed as he quietly drifted into a lonely slumber.

Peter flipped forward through Bobby's book. After watching Bobby torment himself, he almost felt ashamed for the little smile peering from the side of his mouth. He turned through several more chapters and read the next page he stopped on. Peter materialized in a dark alley and saw Bobby walking down the street, barely visible through the shadows. Peter looked around, not recognizing the part of town he was in. The air smelled stale, and the buildings around him seemed abandoned. There were no sounds of family, no lights showing warmth or activity in any of the windows. Peter followed Bobby as he stumbled into a bar and slouched onto a stool.

"What d'ya want?" asked a burly bartender.

"Scotch, neat," Bobby answered without looking. He rubbed the dark stubble on his face and ran his hands through his greasy hair.

The bartender didn't move, he just stared at Bobby. Peter noticed that Bobby's clothes were tattered and stained. The bartender was used to guys like this swigging down their drinks and running out of his bar without paying. He'd worked in this dump far too long to let some bum like this stiff him on a drink.

"That's four bucks up front," he snarled at Bobby. "I ain't no charity."

Bobby looked up, barely able to see through his drunken haze. Squinting at the bartender, Bobby reached into his coat pocket and pulled out two crumpled up dollar bills and slapped them on the bar. He reached into his other pocket and scattered some loose change next to the bills.

"Is that enough for you?" he asked.

The bartender scooped up the money, put a dirty glass in front of Bobby, and poured him half a glass of scotch.

"You're short," he said, turning away from Bobby and throwing the money into the cash register.

Bobby laughed to himself and gulped down the scotch. It stung as it made its way down his throat, but he welcomed the pain. It was the only thing he felt anymore. He searched his pockets for more money. They were as empty as the glass sitting before him, so he pushed himself off his barstool and stumbled his way to the door. As he reached for the doorknob, he heard the bartender mutter.

"Ya bum."

Bobby turned his head slightly and snickered when he heard this.

"Talk like that makes me miss my old man," he told the bartender.

Bobby cinched up the coat around his neck and stepped into the damp night. He staggered down the street and stopped a short way up the sidewalk. Peter watched as he looked up into the sky, almost as though he was trying to find an answer. A shattering crash of a bottle was the last thing Bobby heard before a sharp pain shot through his head, and he fell onto the street, face first into a puddle, with shards of broken glass all around him.

"Check for a wallet," he heard a voice say.

Somebody was shoving their hands into Bobby's pockets.

"This bum ain't got nothing."

"Well, just take his coat then!"

Bobby's coat was stripped off and he was left lying in the puddle, wondering if he'd drown if he didn't move. He heard the footsteps of his unknown attackers scampering off into the distance. Not caring whether he lived or died, Bobby crawled to the alley where Peter stood watching. Bobby felt a warm flow of liquid run down his face. He touched his head, and through the dimly lit night, he noticed the bright red color on his hand as blood trickled down his scalp. Peter watched as Bobby smiled at the sight.

"I guess I deserved that," he said, and then laughed out loud.

Still smiling and looking at his hand, Bobby stood up and walked over to a trashcan. He rummaged through it and retrieved an old, dingy shirt. As he dabbed his head with it, a crumpled-up piece of paper fell out of the pocket and on to the ground. Bobby stopped dabbing his head and picked it up.

"What's this?" he mumbled, walking closer to a streetlight to get a better look. "Hmph, a lottery ticket, huh?"

Then a thought crossed his mind.

"Maybe this one is good for a few bucks. Maybe enough to get me one more drink for the night," he said as he threw the shirt onto the ground and made his way towards a local mini-mart.

The clerk at the store ignored Bobby as this broken-down shadow of a figure staggered into the store.

"Hey," Bobby said as he slapped the ticket onto the counter. "This good for anything?"

Barely looking up from his magazine, the clerk reached under the thick Plexiglas window and took the ticket. When he ran it through the machine, a horn pierced through the store, causing the clerk to drop his magazine. Bobby covered his ears, trying to muffle the noise.

"What the heck's that noise for?" Bobby yelled.

"Sir, you won!" the clerk answered.

"Won what?" Bobby asked. "A couple of bucks?"

"More like a couple of million bucks!" the clerk said, shocked.

"What?" Peter yelled as he now found himself back in his section.

He couldn't believe what he'd just read, so he read it again. He threw the book in anger and watched it slide along the marble floor, stopping in the middle of the corridor.

CHAPTER 14
A Chance at Revenge

"How can a guy like that win the lottery?" Peter screamed to the sky. "You have got to be kidding me!"

His voice echoed off the walls in the large, abandoned room.

"I died because of him, and this is how he gets punished?"

Peter was furious, and as his anger grew, he could do nothing more than stand up and pace.

"He was never nice to anybody! He tormented me for years! He might as well be guilty of murder, go to jail, get hit by a truck, not win a bunch of money! Where's the justice?"

"Is it justice you are looking for?" a voice asked from the darkness.

Peter stopped pacing and froze as a shiver ran up his spine.

"Who said that?" he asked as he slowly looked around.

"My apologies. I didn't mean to startle you, Peter," said this low, raspy voice.

Peter turned in circles. The voice came from all around him. The fear that surged through Peter had his heart thumping so hard he felt like it was going to beat out of his chest. Then Peter noticed an unusual shadow by one of the bookshelves. What Peter thought was a shadow, was actually a darkly-cloaked figure. The unknown person stepped out from the darkness. He was tall but slender, and his face was hidden in the dark brown cloak he wore. Peter could not see his feet or his hands; his cloak hung low and covered both. There was no movement in his legs as he made his way over to Peter. The unknown figure glided above the floor. Stopping in front of Bobby's book, he picked it up off the ground. It was then that Peter noticed the gray skin of the stranger's hand, which clung tightly against each bone in his hand, and as he held the book, Peter noticed that the cover began to age. The once bright gold lettering faded, and the cover frayed where the stranger's hand held it. The soft, raspy voice spoke to Peter.

"Forgive me for not introducing myself."

His eyes were still concealed by the cloak, but he appeared to be staring at the cover of Bobby's book.

"I am Apius."

"Do, do you work in the library?" Peter asked him nervously.

"No, no. I work where no others desire to."

"Oh. Um, I'm Peter."

"Yes, I know," Apius said, barely moving his attention away from Bobby's book. "You are almost infamous here."

"What do you mean?" Peter asked.

Apius continued to stare at the book as he slowly moved around Peter. To him, Apius seemed to be doing more than just looking at the book; he was almost looking *into* the book. His stare was intense, almost like he was studying each page, each word. Apius turned Bobby's book over, and as it turned, it continued to deteriorate in front of Peter's eyes. Strips of leather grayed with age and withered away from the pressboard cover. Apius was now standing directly in front of Peter, staring into his eyes. Peter noticed that Apius's eyes were almost glowing from the deep recess of his shadowed hood.

"Well a boy so young, placed here by a boy so sinister, so evil," he said with a slight laugh, the corners of his mouth barely noticeable as they lifted slightly in amusement.

Peter searched the darkness of Apius's hood for some glimpse of recognition for who stood before him, but only able to see disgusting black and yellow teeth as Apius smiled at him.

"And now you see how that boy, that Bobby, as you call him, was rewarded for his treachery."

Apius tossed the book onto a nearby table. Peter watched as it landed with a thud, which echoed down the hall. Now free from Apius's grip, the book returned to its previous state, complete with shiny gold letters and a clean, pristine leather cover protecting the pages inside. Apius quickly turned to Peter, hesitated for a moment, and then drifted up to him. Peter's fear grew as he took several steps backward.

"He wins all this money. Now, where is the fairness in that?" Apius asked.

"Yeah, well, there's nothing I can do about that now," Peter grumbled.

"Well, I wouldn't say that," chuckled Apius.

"What can I do?" asked Peter. "*Is* there something I can do?"

"Well, it's not really by the rules, but I dare say neither is having this loathsome creature named Bobby winning a great deal of money now is it?"

"Well, I guess not but–"

"Anyway," Apius said as he interrupted Peter, "there is very rare, very special ink that these people do not speak of. It has powers to match that of the Nabi. I have happened upon an occasion to obtain a jar of this ink."

Apius slowly reached into his cloak and pulled out a crystal ink jar similar to the ones the Nabi used. However, contained inside this jar wasn't the brilliant gold ink Peter was accustomed to seeing. This ink was a deep crimson color, with what appeared to be thousands of tiny rubies suspended inside. Apius held the jar in his hand, just beyond Peter's reach.

"This particular ink can also be used to lead a person's life, to alter that which is already written," Apius paused and watched as Peter stared at the ink jar.

"I feel your anger, Peter, and wish only to help. To stop the suffering you live with day after day. To give you back some happiness, like that which you enjoyed so long ago."

Peter stood there, unable to speak, uncertain of how he felt.

"Perhaps I could allow you to take possession of this rare treasure and fix this heinous error," Apius sneered.

"I, I don't think I could do anything like that," Peter said as he continued to stare at the jar.

"Pity," Apius said, sullen, as he withdrew his hand.

But as he turned away, Peter's hand cautiously trailed after the jar. Seeing this made Apius smile.

"However," he said, turning back to Peter, "you don't have to use this precious gift at all, but it's nice to know you could if you wanted to, isn't it? Don't you feel better already, just having that bit of knowledge? Knowing that ink with a power such as this exists? Don't you feel at ease knowing you can correct this injustice with a stroke of your hand? If you chose to do so, of course."

"Sure, but I–"

"Mmmmm, look, Peter," Apius said with a sense of levity in his voice. "You have enough pressure here already. These people push you and push you. Turn those pages. All of the pages must be turned before the clock chimes and all that nonsense!" Apius said, waving his hands about angrily until he calmed his voice again. "I am not here to pressure you, Peter. I would never pressure you. Let me just place this ink jar back here, right behind this shelf, where only you and I know about. If you choose to use it, then you will know where to find it."

He bent over and set the ink jar down on one of the lower shelves. Apius watched Peter's expression as his long, pale, scaly finger pushed it behind the shadows of the books. Peter listened as the crystal jar slowly scratched its way across the wooden shelf. Apius stood up and stared at the spot he had just hidden the jar in. Peter was staring at it, too, which caused Apius to smile.

"It will be here if you need it, Peter," he said as he walked away. "If you don't, then just forget about it," Apius then turned to Peter. "Bobby will go on with his glorious, wealthy life. He will be smiling and laughing about being dirty rich as you lay beneath the dirt."

Apius snickered as he said this, but Peter found no humor in what he said and his anger resurfaced.

"You take care, Peter," Apius said as he turned to leave, but then turned back to Peter and pointed his slender finger toward the shelves.

"Ahh yes, don't forget to finish turning those pages," he told Peter with a soft, raspy laugh.

Peter looked back at the shelf where the ink jar was hidden, and then he turned to Apius.

"How do I—?"

However, Apius had already disappeared into the darkness.

Peter looked at the tapestry. The door was no longer there. Now Peter was left alone, staring at the shelf where the ink jar was hidden. Even though he couldn't see it, Peter somehow still felt its presence, almost as if someone was still in the room with him. He walked up to the shelf, slowly, cautiously, and when he got to the spot where Apius had hidden it, Peter crouched down, carefully reached behind the shelf, and grabbed the jar. When he pulled it out, he noticed a small card tied around the neck. There were words written on the card, but he had to move below a nearby candle to make the curved scribbling out. Once he was able to see, he read the words out loud.

"The words that are written can cause a boy's dismay.

Only to be changed with this ink in a day.

Scratch through the lines, which are causing you ill.

Replace them carefully, with determination, and a Nabi's quill."

Peter stood silent for a moment, focused on the card in his hand. Great. All he had to do was find a Nabi's quill. But how the heck was he supposed to get one of those? Peter brought the jar over to a nearby table.

"It should be easy enough." He tried convincingly telling himself.

He sat down and stared at the jar, wondering if he could actually change Bobby's life. Even though Bobby had done some rotten, cruel things to him, he was having a hard time justifying his revenge. Since the first day he'd learned about the LifeBooks, he'd been told how important they were, and how carefully they were written and handled.

"What should I do?" he whispered as he picked up the jar.

It was surprising how warm it felt in his hands, and as he sat there in the shadows of the flickering candlelight staring at it, Peter's thoughts drifted to Bobby. He thought back on all of the lies he'd told his parents in order to hide his embarrassment and shame. How Bobby had tied Peter's new backpack to his bike and dragged it up and down the street until it was a tattered mess. How he'd hit Peter in the head with a milk carton in the cafeteria for the amusement of his cronies. All the time, Peter had remained quiet, never telling his parents of the torment he endured. Hiding all of the cuts, the bruises, the tears with one lie after the next.

"And for what!" Peter screamed.

The angrier he got, the warmer the jar got.

"It wasn't just me," he said, gritting his teeth as he glared at the jar. "All of those other kids Bobby pushed around, what happened to them? Where is their justice?"

Peter loosened his grip and his eyebrows raised.

"Mom, dad," he whispered as his lip started to quiver.

He thought about the pain they'd had to go through each and every day; he pictured his mother on the porch as the police arrived to tell her what had happened to her little boy. How she must have felt when she got the news. He could imagine his father rushing up the driveway to see Peter, but now only seeing his empty room.

Looking down, he noticed that his hand was once again white from gripping the jar so tight, so he set it down on the table. The jar wasn't just hot, it was now sparkling.

Peter couldn't remember the last time he'd felt this angry. He rested his chin on top of his hands as he took a deep breath, hoping it would help him calm down. After catching his breath, he stood up and returned the jar to its hiding place behind the shelf. The night had turned late, and he was exhausted. Hoping everyone was in bed by now, he returned to his room where he spent his time lying in his bed, staring at the ceiling, his head full of thoughts on how to get even with Bobby. Even though he came up with a dozen different scenarios he could write in Bobby's book, he felt guilty about the plans he was fantasizing about. Regardless of the hate and anger raging inside of him, Peter wasn't sure he was the type of person to seek out revenge.

Nonetheless, Peter happily spent the next several hours obsessing over it, yet struggling to convince himself that he wasn't this type of person. As the hours passed, no matter how hard he tried, Peter couldn't make himself forget about the opportunity being given to him. His thoughts of innocence and forgiveness slowly disappeared and were replaced by thoughts of revenge.

"I wouldn't be doing this for myself. That would be selfish. I'm doing this for all the kids Bobby picked on."

A creak at the door distracted him for a brief moment before he turned his attention back to his thoughts.

"Not even just Bobby. This is for all of those bullies out there. It wouldn't be wrong to at least correct the unfair things written in Bobby's book. I mean, c'mon, winning the lottery? Who'd want something like that to happen to a guy like this?"

With all these thoughts running through his head, there was no way Peter was going to get any sleep, so he got out of bed and made his way back to his section. At this time of night, the halls were darker and colder than normal. As he skulked his way into his section, he went over to the table where Apius had thrown Bobby's book. Nobody was there, but Bobby's book still was, its gold letters almost taunting Peter. He picked the book up and stared at it.

"No, I can't," he said, squeezing his eyes shut and shaking his head, but when he went to put it down, he couldn't let go.

"Fine," he grunted after several tries.

Scowling, Peter pulled out a pillowcase he'd smuggled in with him and quickly slid Bobby's LifeBook inside of it before tucking it back underneath his shirt. Peter's heart raced as he made his way back to his room, constantly looking around for anyone else. He shut the door and ensured it was locked before setting his precious cargo onto the bed. As an extra precaution, he walked over to the windows, pulled the curtains closed, and turned off all of the lights except for his desk lamp. As soon as he picked up the pillowcase, Peter felt his anger flowing through him again. He pulled the book from the sack, and his grip tightened as he stood staring at the name on the cover once more. He'd never thought the sight of a book would stir up so much hate and rage in him.

"Ugh!" he yelled, dropping the book onto the desk.

Hoping to clear his head, Peter walked over to the window to get some fresh air. When he pulled back the curtains, he saw that the once calm ocean had turned into a violent storm. The more he thought about Bobby, the more rage he felt, and the stronger the wind and waves of the ocean became until a hurricane set in. The wind whipped through Peter's room, tossing everything off the shelves. The cold ocean spray stung his face, but Peter wasn't afraid; he stood there, smiling. He reveled at the power and turmoil that the storm created. Watching the cresting waves crash over the jagged rocks below, and with every ebb of the ocean, Peter craved the power behind it. Even though he was shivering, the cold spray dripping from his face, he just smiled.

After a few flashes of lightning, he shut the window. The storm had left his room in shambles. Chairs had been knocked over, shelves had fallen, and his mirror had shattered. He stepped over the broken glass, strewn all about and went over to his bed. Wiping the salty water from his face with his blanket, Peter couldn't do anything more than stare at that book.

For what seemed to be hours, he sat there, looking at it, just as Apius had done. Peter still struggled with the idea of what to do. Part of him wanted to throw it in the ocean, but he knew he couldn't do that. If he did, the pages in Bobby's book wouldn't get turned, and everything in the library would come to a halt. They'd certainly have to investigate that. They'd know it was Peter who took the book. The only other options for him were to keep it or to return it to the library and forget about it. If he brought it back to the library, then it could get moved or misplaced. Peter couldn't risk that because then Bobby would win, again, and Peter was tired of Bobby winning.

He paced back and forth for a while until he finally decided to keep the book in his room, but only until he was positive of the plan he should follow. He took the book over to his dresser where he hid it next to the wall. Peter thought he'd be able to think more clearly after a good night's rest. He could then choose whether or not he should change what the Nabi had written.

CHAPTER 15
Peter's Struggle With Fate

Peter woke up in a foul mood. All he could picture was Bobby sitting on a beach enjoying all of his money, and on top of that, he couldn't find his parent's picture. Nonetheless, that wasn't Peter's focus any longer. Immediately, he went behind his dresser to make sure Bobby's book was still there. When he reached his hand down and felt the course leather of the LifeBook, Peter had mixed emotions. Part of him had hoped it was a dream, that Bobby hadn't actually won the lottery, and another part of him seethed with excitement that he could change Bobby's life to a more miserable existence. Peter spent the next several hours cleaning his room, still at odds over what to do. Lifting up a shelf that had fallen from the wall, he found his parent's picture beneath the clutter. He took a moment to look at it lying on the floor before heading off to lunch.

He didn't do much else that day. Even though he tried to have fun and explore, his focus had vanished and had succumbed to his inner demons. Innocence turned to paranoia as he worried about someone finding the ink jar.

Dinner came and went as Peter sat in his room, watching the sun slowly disappear behind the ocean. Hoping to better his mood, he went over to his bed and watched as the room transformed itself. Seeing his own bedroom reminded him of the good times when he was home with his parents, but even this couldn't snap him out of his sullen demeanor.

"What if some nosey helper starts poking around and they find it?" he asked, warily scanning the room. "Worst yet, did somebody come by today to clean the shelves? Do they even clean the shelves?"

His eyes darted back and forth across the ceiling.

"Argh! I'll never get to sleep now!" he grumbled as he jumped out of bed and ran to the Conservatory.

As he passed the fountain, he paused to stare at the sign above the door to his section.

Section III

Who knew how many times he'd passed through these doors. Now, just beyond them was the key to get back at Bobby for all the years of torment. Peter stood still at the entrance, knowing that tonight if he stepped through it, there would be no turning back. Without any further hesitation, he marched straight into his section and over to the spot where the jar was hidden. He reached behind the shelf and was relieved to feel the etched glass of the jar. Peter pulled it out, and after looking around to make sure he was alone, he placed it into his pocket and went back to his room.

"Stupid ink," he muttered as he slammed the jar onto his nightstand before burrowing himself underneath his blanket.

Of all the things Peter could be doing, he certainly wasn't interested in turning pages that next morning. With each day that passed, he laggardly performed his task while becoming more fixated on taking Bobby's book and changing his so-called good fortune. Just momentarily thinking about it made Peter mad, and he got even angrier when he found he couldn't stop thinking about it. So mad in fact, that as he got dressed, muttering angry wishes on Bobby, he yanked his sock onto his foot so hard that his big toe tore a hole into the end of it. Even so, it didn't faze him. He just pulled his shoe on and headed out of his room.

"Ugh!" he grunted as he walked back into his room, grabbed the ink jar with a sneer, and secreted it next to Bobby's book. "I'm miserable," he grumbled. "So what makes Bobby so special that he can't be miserable too?"

His thoughts drifted back and forth. What Bobby did to him and what Peter could do to get even with him was all that mattered right now. The more he thought about Bobby, the more disgusted he got. He was in no mood for pleasantries today, and as he walked down the hallway, he made sure to stay out of everyone's way. All he wanted to do was finish his work. Getting to the Conservatory, he didn't look up to see who was around; he just kept staring at the floor, all the time grunting and sneering.

"Who does Bobby think he is anyways? Probably out buying himself a new bike or beating up a kid on his way to baseball practice," Peter said as he clenched his fingers into a fist.

He shoved the doors of his section open, causing them to slam into the wall and several people to jump.

"What am I waiting for?" he groused as he pushed the ladder to the beginning of his section.

As he climbed up the ladder, he heard a noise that caused him to stop. It sounded like someone laughing over in the corner of the room.

"Hmph," Peter grunted as he dismissed the noise and continued to climb the ladder. "Probably just Bobby laughing at me in that book of his. Having a great old time, I'm sure. Now he's just laughing at me all over again. Just like he used to."

As he continued to turn the pages of the LifeBooks, his mood remained awful. A grumbling in his stomach reminded him it was time to eat. Lunchtime used to be one of his favorite times of day; now it didn't receive the attention from Peter that an ant would merit walking past him. He jammed the book he held back into its place on the shelf, walked over to the entrance of his section, and pulled the doors open so hard they made the same echoing boom as when he'd first arrived. His fists were clenched tight as he walked down the hall. Miss Penntiworth approached him from the other end of the hall, carrying a stack of papers.

"Good afternoon, Peter," she said as he passed her.

"Hmph," he murmured as he walked past her, still looking at the ground.

Miss Penntiworth was too caught up in reading and didn't notice Peter's demeanor.

"Gotta hurry up and eat lunch so I can spend the rest of my day turning those stupid pages," he muttered. "Hate for someone to miss their fun today."

That reminded Peter of something extremely important. Once he was finished turning all of the pages he was responsible for, he also had to make certain he turned the pages in Bobby's book. If not, somebody might come looking for it. If they did and found out Peter had been hiding it all of this time, it would ruin everything. So instead of eating lunch, Peter went back to his room to turn the page in Bobby's book before he forgot. As with every other door that was in his way today, Peter yanked open the door to his bedroom and slammed it shut. He walked over to his dresser, pulled out Bobby's book, and tossed it onto his bed.

"Hope you're doing ok today, Bobby," he said as he reached down and threw the book open, then moved the marker out of the way.

Peter slapped his hand onto the page and flipped it over. He wasn't concerned whether the page ripped, crumpled, or came right out of the book as he put the page marker back in place and slammed the book shut.

"Well I hope you enjoy your day, Bobby," he snarled before reaching behind the dresser and jamming the book back into its hiding spot. "Probably gonna go buy himself a baseball team or something," he sneered as he stormed out of his room and went back to his section.

Ever since he'd come across Bobby's book, things had grown worse than ever for Peter.

Once his job was finished, he'd walk past the cafeteria without even a second look. He no longer craved his mealtime adventures. It was now a rarity that Peter even thought about his parents or spent time talking to Miss Penntiworth. All he could do was think about Bobby's LifeBook. He was obsessed!

Peter finished working and immediately went to his room. After storming in, he walked over to the window and closed the drapes without even acknowledging the fisherman casting his line into the sea. He retrieved the jar and spent the next several hours staring at it.

The longer Peter stared at the jar, the more he forgot about the other things around him. His rage had engulfed him, and the joy he'd received from his travels and adventures was replaced by this tiny jar of thick red liquid. He knew every inch of that jar, from the etched crystal dragons encircling it to the discolored tan and black cork sealing its contents. Peter spent all of his free time staring at the jar. He was at a crossroads in his life and didn't even realize it.

"Why don't I just change this stupid book?" he asked. "What am I waiting for? Better yet, where am I going to get a stinking Nabi's quill to even use this stuff?"

Peter wondered if he should just give the jar back to Apius and forget about the whole thing. The back and forth of this decision was overwhelming. Even though he didn't know what direction to take, he felt as though he needed to do something soon. With each passing day, Peter was becoming more and more paranoid, and now he rarely left his room. His eyes darkened, and his hair grew more disheveled than it used to be. When he did eat, he didn't do anything more than pick the first book he came across, ate whatever they were serving, and came directly back to his room, where he would spend the rest of the time pacing and talking to himself.

"People are starting to notice," he muttered as he walked back and forth in front of the ink jar sitting on his nightstand. "It won't be long before that Penntiworth lady trespasses in here and demands me to do something like eat with her or talk about my feelings," he hissed.

He stopped for a moment and stared at the door as though he was waiting for her to walk through it. When nobody came in, he frowned and went back to grousing.

"Who does she think she is anyways, my mother?" he growled, but then stopped pacing for a moment as his forehead raised.

"My mom," he whispered.

She distracted Peter from his rage. He now felt sad thinking about her.

"I miss her so much."

He stopped staring at the jar and looked up at the ceiling. His thoughts turned to his parents as he walked over to the clutter on the floor and grabbed their photograph. As he sat on his bed, he remembered how he used to wait for them to come tuck him in at night. How he would wake up on Saturdays and smell the sweet scent of fresh waffles his mom made especially for him.

Peter stood up and walked over to the window. He slid the drapes open and noticed that the fisherman was still in the boat, but he wasn't fishing. He was staring up at Peter. Peter tried to make out the man's face, wondering if he knew what Peter was up to, but after several moments, the man tipped his hat to Peter and went back to his fishing. Peter half-heartedly waved back, wondering if people were starting to suspect something.

CHAPTER 16
His Chance

When Peter woke up, he couldn't find the jar, which sent him into a panic! His heart raced as he ran over to his dresser. Once he reached beneath and felt the etchings, he breathed out a sigh of relief and dislodged it from its spot.

"How did you get back here?" he asked, turning the jar between his fingers. "Even if I want to use you, I still have to get a Nabi's quill."

So, there he sat for the next several hours trying to figure out how he could get one of the quills without anyone noticing, but none of the ideas he came up with seemed as though they would work. Frustrated, he went back and slid the ink jar back into its spot once more.

"Maybe I *should* just forget the whole thing," he said, staring at his dresser. "But the only thing missing is that quill," he kept repeating to himself.

"I've got to get out of this room," he said, hoping that some fresh air would help to clear his head. "Maybe that will help shake something loose so I can come up with a good plan."

As soon as Peter stepped into the hallway, he looked up and saw Miss Penntiworth coming his way.

"Oh, good morning, Peter, I've been looking for you," she said.

Peter had a lot to deal with, and he didn't have time to exchange pleasantries. So, he smiled and nodded, hoping that would be enough for her and she'd continue on her way. Unfortunately, she stopped directly in front of him.

"Good morning, Miss Penntiworth," he said, almost under his breath, purposely avoiding eye contact with her, hoping she would pick up on this and know that he did not feel like talking today.

"Peter, is there any chance that you could help me out with something today?" she asked.

"Uh, yeah sure, I guess," he muttered.

"I was wondering if you might help out in the Nabi's room?"

Peter perked up. This was exactly the opportunity he needed to help him get his hands on a quill! "Of course!" he said enthusiastically.

"Terrific! Why don't we head over there now so I can show you what I need you to do," she told him.

This put him in a much better mood, and as he and Miss Penntiworth made their way to the Nabi's room, Miss Penntiworth gave him some instructions. Unfortunately for Peter, he was barely listening, focused on finalizing his plan.

Okay, so first I have to try to take one of their quills. Then, I have to somehow get it out of the room before anyone notices.

"Ah, here we are," Miss Penntiworth said, opening the door.

As they entered the room, it was as dark and cold as Peter remembered, but he couldn't be bothered with that right now. His eyes darted around the room as he tried to come up with his plan.

"Now, Peter, unlike the Conservatory, you will have to do this job every day, but this job takes much less time. It is really simple, because all you need to do is–"

She continued to explain the job to him, but his mind had already drifted, and he didn't hear a word she said.

Stay focused you dummy, he told himself as he tried forcing himself to pay attention. As she continued on, Peter hoped she'd just hurry up and finish so she would leave. Once she was gone, he could formulate a plan to get the quill, and every moment she spoke was another moment wasted.

Miss Penntiworth finally stopped talking long enough for him to nod his head in agreement. He wasn't sure what he was nodding for, but it seemed to work since she smiled at him, rubbed his head, and walked out of the room.

This was his chance.

He walked over to the door with her and waited until she disappeared down the hall and around the corner. Once he was certain she was far enough away, Peter scurried around, hoping to find a discarded quill on the floor. Unfortunately, he found nothing more than handfuls of moss. Reluctantly, he walked up to one of the Nabi. This being, as it were, was scratching words across the page, totally ignoring Peter.

"Maybe it won't even notice if I just take this thing," he said as he reached forward and snatched the quill out of the Nabi's hand.

The instant that Peter removed the quill, the Nabi leaned back, dropped its jaw and opened its mouth so wide, Peter felt he could almost crawl inside. The Nabi then let out a high-pitched screech that pierced through the cold and darkness of the room. Peter covered his ears, ran over to the door, and leaned against it to make certain that nobody entered.

"Someone is definitely going to hear this noise!" he yelled as he ran back and put the quill back into that Nabi's hand.

As soon as he did, the screeching stopped, and the Nabi went back to scratching words across the page, seemingly unaffected by everything that had just taken place. Peter winced as he rubbed his ears and then looked back at the door. Nobody had come in, so he walked over, opened it slightly, and peeked outside.

"Maybe nobody heard it," he whispered, relieved not to see anyone in the hallway. After quietly closing the door, he resumed his search for a quill. "There has to be a spare one lying around somewhere," he whispered.

But as he looked around the room, there were no quills other than the ones the Nabi were holding. With all of that screeching, Peter couldn't figure out how he was going to get one of them away from the Nabi and get out of there without anyone noticing. And if somebody did notice, there was no way he'd have enough time to change Bobby's book before they caught him.

"There has to be another way," he whispered as he continued to look around the room.

Since he couldn't find another quill, Peter wandered the room until he noticed that one of the Nabi had completed his book. He watched the Nabi close the book, put the quill on the table, and then stare ahead, motionless. Peter remembered seeing this when he first visited the room. Miss Penntiworth said they would do this until somebody brought them a new book. Peter cautiously walked over to the table and stood in front of the Nabi. There was no reaction. Even after waving his hands in front of its face, it just ignored him and continued to stare straight ahead. Peter carefully reached forward and took the quill that lay on the table. After he'd picked it up, he cringed as he waited for the shriek, but there was none.

"That's it!" He smiled, knowing this was the answer he'd been looking for. "All I have to do is wait for one of them to finish writing. Then I can take the quill for as long as I need it."

Or so he thought. The problem he now faced was that someone would surely be bringing the Nabi another book. Peter wondered how much time he'd have before a helper appeared. There weren't any clocks around, so Peter decided to keep count in his head as he waited.

"One potato, two potatoes, three potatoes…" he counted.

Peter got to forty-five potatoes before a helper came in. She smiled at Peter as she brought in the new book and took the completed one with her. Ten potatoes later, another helper came in and gave the Nabi a new ink jar.

Too many people. Peter thought. *And forty-five potatoes isn't long enough to get back at Bobby.*

Peter paced around the room again, questions filling his head. When the helpers brought in the new book and ink, they'd certainly notice the Nabi's quill was missing, wouldn't they? Or even if they didn't, once the new book was in front of the Nabi, wouldn't it start screeching again because the quill was gone and it couldn't write?

There were too many unknowns. Peter didn't feel comfortable with this plan, so he was going to have to figure out a way to keep the helpers out of the room. This would allow him time to get the quill and leave. He would also need enough time to change at least a few things in Bobby's book. The only problem was keeping the helpers from coming in. As he struggled through this problem, it dawned on him that he was supposed to be doing something for Miss Penntiworth.

"Great!" he yelled. "What am I supposed to be doing in here?"

Now he was upset with himself that he hadn't listened to her. Since he was unsure of what he was supposed to be doing, and he didn't know how long he'd been with the Nabi, he went back to his room. Maybe tomorrow, Miss Penntiworth would ask him what happened and give him some sort of clue.

The next day, Peter was on his way back to the Nabi's room when he ran into Miss Penntiworth in the hallway.

"Well, good morning, Peter," she said.

"Um, good morning," he answered nervously.

He'd thought about it all night, but he still couldn't remember what he was supposed to be doing in the Nabi's room.

"Did you have any trouble finding out where to put the completed books?" she asked Peter.

That was it, he thought.

He now knew why the woman yesterday had given him a weird look when she dropped off the new book.

"No, no trouble at all," he told her.

"That's wonderful, Peter, and I really appreciate you helping out. Do you think it would be possible for you to keep doing this for a short while longer?" she asked.

This is perfect, Peter thought. "No, Miss. Penntiworth," he said, smiling. "If this helps you out, I am more than happy to do it."

"Wonderful! Thank you so much, Peter. You are such a dear. Now if you will excuse me, I have to run and meet Mr. Grumsby. You know how he gets when someone is late," she said to Peter as she smiled and rushed away.

Now that Peter knew what his new job was, and he had some extra time in the Nabi's room, all that was left to do was to perfect his plan. Peter smiled as she ran off, but even though everything was starting to come together, it was still not the ideal situation. First of all, he hated going into the Nabi's room. It was an extremely depressing place to be. As soon as he entered the room, the sound of his breathing amplified above the eerie quiet. But this sound was second only to the scratching of quills, which resonated throughout. That was the one thing Peter hated the most. That scratching built up inside your head. It started off as a faint disruption to the silence that otherwise occupied the room. After several minutes, it would start bouncing back and forth in his ears. Peter felt that any prolonged exposure would certainly drive somebody mad.

"I guess I was too busy yesterday to notice," Peter said as he covered his ears.

Instead of waiting to collect all of the finished books at once, he thought he'd gather each one up as soon as the Nabi was finished with it. This would allow him to get away from the room and that awful noise. However, Peter still didn't know where the books needed to go. So, as he sat there waiting for one of them to finish, he removed his socks and made a crude set of earmuffs by balling them up and tying them into place with his shoelaces. Peter then spent a good amount of time sitting and staring at the Nabi. They still creeped him out, but he was somewhat fascinated by them. The Nabi were almost robotic in their movements. He was amazed at the routine of their work; nothing distracted them.

"Hmm," he said as he stood up and walked over to one of the tables, thinking he would try something out.

But even when Peter pounded his fist on the table, the Nabi did not flinch. They just kept writing in their books. Peter was getting ready to climb up on the table to jump up and down when he heard the echo of footsteps coming toward the room. He walked over to one of the Nabi that had completed his writing and picked up the book in front of him. An elderly woman walked into the room with a clean book for the Nabi.

"Good morning," she said to Peter with a puzzled look on her face.

"Hi, good morning," he replied, looking like he had big dog ears from the socks.

She put the book in front of the Nabi, and as she started to walk out, Peter stopped her.

"Excuse me, I'm sorry," Peter said. "I kind of forgot what I'm supposed to do with these books?"

She smiled at Peter.

"Not a problem at all," she said. "Follow me."

She led him out into the hallway and pointed to a set of double doors at the end of the hall.

"Just go through those doors. There's a sign above the entrance that says 'Repository'," she explained to him. "On the left, you will see a number of carts lined up along the wall. All you have to do is place the book on one of those carts. Once one is full of books, you need to take it to the Conservatory. Someone will take it from you there."

"Thank you so much," he said to her.

"Anytime, son."

He waited for her to leave before walking down the hall to where she'd directed him. Through the double doors, there were carts lined up along the wall like she'd said. Peter also noticed two arched alcoves nearby. One contained several shelves with the ink jars. The other contained shelves with blank books lined up neatly. There was a tiny brass bell above each alcove. As he gazed on, the one above the ink jar alcove rang. Peter watched as an assistant came in and grabbed an ink jar off the shelf then walked down the hall and went into one of the Nabi's room.

"Interesting," he said as he made his way back to his room.

Peter spent the rest of the day going back and forth from the Repository to the Nabi's room. He was getting a better understanding of how things worked, but he was still struggling to come up with an idea of how to get a quill and keep it long enough to make his changes.

At one point during the day, Peter realized that he'd not yet eaten and was starving. He had been so busy all day that he didn't even notice if lunchtime had come yet or not. An older boy walked up to Peter.

"Hey, I'm here to relieve you," he told Peter.

"Great, I could use some lunch," he said.

"Yeah, um, it's dinner time kid," the boy said.

Peter couldn't believe it. He'd gone through the whole day without even realizing he'd missed lunch. As he made his way to the cafeteria, he tried to figure out which book to use for dinner. It had been quite some time since he had an appetite, but now, with all the excitement to get a quill momentarily paused, Peter was hungry. He settled on going back to the diner where he'd seen his parents before. After walking into the cafeteria, he went over and found the book where he'd purposely left it. As he opened the book and read the all too familiar line, he found himself immediately looking around for his mom and dad. They weren't there, so he took some time to sit there and reflect on the times he and his parents had spent there.

"These used to be such good times," he said.

He sat silently for some time before asking for something to eat. There was only one thing Peter wanted, and it was the tuna fish casserole. After ordering a large plate of casserole, he watched the people come in and out of the restaurant as he ate. Every now and then a family would come in, and Peter would spend most of his time watching the interaction between the parents and the kids. This made him sad, and he now realized what Emily had been telling him. He couldn't go home this way. It became torturous for him to watch this. If he had to see his parents spending time with some other kid, it would be awful. This realization made him angry, and his anger turned to Bobby. Once he returned to the cafeteria, Peter knew what he must do.

CHAPTER 17
Hidden in A Dark Corner

Several weeks had passed since Peter started helping out in the Nabi's room. In the Conservatory, time normally passed unnoticed, but Peter knew he'd been in his new position a while when he actually recognized some of the other helpers who brought the Nabi their books and ink. Even though, he still hadn't come up with a decent idea of how to get a quill, and as Peter left his room trying to devise his plan, he ran into Miss Penntiworth.

"Oh good, I'm glad I ran into you, Peter. I wanted to let you know that today will be the last day you have to help out in the Nabi's room. We have somebody new who will be starting there tomorrow," she told him.

Peter's heart stopped! *This is no good*, he thought. He smiled nervously, unsure what he was going to do. He had to come up with something quick if he was going to finish this.

"Oh?" said Peter. "It really isn't a problem, Miss Penntiworth. As a matter of fact, if you want this person to take over my section, I could continue to work in the Nabi's room."

"That's very sweet of you, dear, but I know you don't like it in there. You were a wonderful boy for helping me out, and I appreciate it, but I couldn't ask you to spend any more time in there than you have to."

Peter wanted to insist on working there, but after all of his previous complaining, he worried it would make her suspicious. He had to come up with a plan...fast.

"Okay, well if you need anything, you know where to find me," he told her as he hurried off.

"Wonderful, Peter. Thank you again."

When Peter got to the room, he noticed that one of the books was completed, so he immediately picked it up and headed to the

Repository. After putting the book on a cart, he recognized one of the girls who'd recently been coming to the Nabi's room. She was tall, slightly older than Peter, and wore thick glasses. She was carrying a new LifeBook and ink jar to the Nabi's room, her long ponytail swinging back and forth like an out of control pendulum. An idea popped into Peter's head.

"Hey," he said to her.

"Hi. Are you still working in the Nabi's room?" she asked.

"Yeah, still there," he frowned. "My name is Peter by the way."

"Hi, I'm Christine. I give you a lot of credit. That place gives me the willies," she said, looking down the darkened hall.

"Yeah, it kind of does that to you," he said as he stared at the book in her hand.

"I don't have much longer doing this," she told Peter with a smile. "I'm supposed to go to work in the Conservatory and collect the completed books. I'm so looking forward to that. The Conservatory is so beautiful; plus it'll keep me out of here."

"Oh, good for you," he said. "You know, I'm going back to the Nabi's room right now. I could take that stuff for you," he told her. "At least it will keep you out of there for one more trip."

"That would be great," Christine said. "You don't mind?"

"No, not at all. I have to go back there anyways," he told her, motioning his head to the room.

"That's awesome," she said. "It probably seems kind of silly to you."

"Not at all," he said with a big cunning smile on his face. "I'm happy to help out."

Christine gave Peter the book and ink, then rubbed his arm.

"I really appreciate you doing this. If I don't see you again, take care."

"You, too." He smiled as Christine walked off.

This is great! he thought. *This could buy me some extra time with a quill.*

He ran into the Nabi's room to make sure none of them were close to finishing any of their books. When Peter was satisfied that it would be some time before another book was finished, he hid the new LifeBook and ink jar in the darkest corner he could find, doing his best to cover up the glow from the ink behind the book. When he was satisfied it was hidden, Peter walked up to the Nabi who was sitting there, patiently waiting. As he reached for the quill, he hesitated. He wasn't sure why he was nervous to take it.

"He didn't scream last time," he whispered as he took a deep breath and then quickly grabbed the quill.

He stood there cringing with his eyes closed, and just as before, the Nabi stayed quiet. Peter smiled and ran out of the room, headed to his bedroom as fast as he could go. The thought of Bobby was gnawing at Peter the whole way. When he got to his room, he flung the door open and ran to the dresser where the book hid in the shadows of his drawer. Peter took it out and looked at it for a moment before there was a knock at the door. Peter's heart jumped into his throat.

"Peter, are you all right?" asked Miss Penntiworth.

Just as she opened the door, Peter slid the book underneath his shirt.

"I'm sorry to barge in here dear. I saw you run into here and you looked distressed, so I wanted to check on you."

"No, no. I'm fine, thanks." Peter awkwardly answered.

"Good. I'm sorry to have disturbed you. Let me know if you need anything." she told him as she walked out and closed the door.

Peter's heart started beating again.

"I can't risk that again," he said as he grabbed the ink jar, stuffed it into his pocket and made his way to the Conservatory.

Several people were still working in his section when he got there, so he made extra sure that the book was still concealed in his shirt as he walked past them. After he gave several of his coworkers a somewhat awkward smile, he scurried over to the tapestry.

"It's quiet over there," he whispered. "Nobody ever goes over there."

Once he got there, Peter felt as though he was still too much in the open, but he was running out of time. Hoping that the door was still there, he reached for the tapestry and pulled it back. There it was! Peter's heart jumped as he quickly opened the door and crept down the stairs.

"Nobody will bother me down here," he said as he disappeared behind the door, then listened for a moment.

When he was certain that nobody followed him, he descended the stairs. As if on queue, the torches on the walls popped to life with each step, the quivering flames providing a much-needed warmth, which would not last. As he tightly clutched Bobby's book under his arm, he began to shiver, not sure if it was because he was nervous, or because it was getting colder and colder as he descended the seemingly endless staircase. When he got to the bottom, he was surprised to see nothing but a large empty room illuminated by several torches. The floor was nothing more than cold, hard dirt.

Peter walked over to the farthest corner, where he sat down and rubbed his hands together, trying to warm them up. As he opened Bobby's book, the words were barely legible in the flickering light. Even though he wasn't reading, the longer he stared at the pages, the angrier he got. He still couldn't believe how Bobby's life turned out after all of the rotten things that he'd done, not just to Peter, but to dozens of other kids. Peter looked at the ink jar that Apius had given to him, and then he looked back at the book.

"This isn't right. I can't do this," he said as he stood up and went to close Bobby's book, which slipped from his hands and fell to the floor. Peter picked it up and immediately recognized the page that it had flipped to.

"This is the part where Bobby wins the lottery," Peter said as he felt himself getting furious all over again. "Why did he do this to me?" he screamed into the darkness.

Sitting back down, he pulled the cork from the top of the ink jar. As it popped out, Peter heard faint whispers resonate throughout the room.

"Do it. Do it," the voices whispered from all around him. "He deserves it. Are you really going to let him win?"

Peter sat there, listening to the voices and staring at the book as the room became even colder. His breathing turned quick and short, as his breath was a wispy cloud before him. Peter took a moment before he dipped the Nabi's quill into the ink jar, and as he did, he felt his heart race. The deeper Peter lowered the quill into the jar, the warmer it felt in his hand, and the warmth gave him a feeling of reassurance from the bitter cold surrounding him.

"Fine!" he said as he positioned the book on his lap.

The first page Peter changed was the one where Bobby found the lottery ticket. Peter scratched through a line on the page, but his mark slowly disappeared. He tried it again but got the same result. Peter remembered the tag said he also had to replace the words. There was enough space in-between the sentences, so that's what he would do. Peter took the quill and again pressed the sharp point, dripping in ink, against the paper and scratched his words across the pages. Peter watched as the words appeared like they were written in blood. Deep crimson and silent were the words that stared back at Peter.

"As Bobby leaves the convenience store, the same people who had taken his coat come back. They hit Bobby again and steal his lottery ticket," he wrote.

After finishing the last word of his sentence, Bobby's book started to change. Lines that the Nabi had written began to disappear from the pages. Peter did not look forward to see what had happened after the lottery ticket had been stolen away from Bobby, he just continued to the next item eating away at him: Bobby making the baseball team.

As Peter continued to add lines to Bobby's book, he watched some of the pages decay into dust as the book got thinner. Miss Penntiworth's voice suddenly sounded in his head.

"Each event in your life, good or bad, adds or takes away other events. One gives life to another or takes the life away," her voice echoed.

These words didn't matter, though, because Peter was focused on finishing what he'd started. Once he finalized making his own entries in Bobby's book, he closed it and sat there quietly. Everything in the room had gone silent; there was no scratching quill, no whispered voices, even Miss Penntiworth's voice inside his head was gone.

None of that surprised Peter, however. What surprised him was that he felt no excitement. There was no joy in finally getting back at Bobby. The experience wasn't void of emotion altogether, because Peter did feel strange about what he'd done. It was very similar to the feeling he got when he'd sneak candy before dinner. Much like the sound of Miss Penntiworth's voice in his head, Peter shrugged off his thoughts of uncertainty and headed up the stairs.

"After I put Bobby's book back on the shelf, I can go around and check to make sure nobody suspects anything," he muttered. "Then, I'll go and return the Nabi's quill before anybody notices that it's missing."

He got to the top of the stairs and cautiously stuck his head out of the door. After a quick peek from behind the tapestry, it was clear nobody was around, so he slowly stepped out and shut the door before heading into his section. When he got there, he froze. As if a tornado had ripped through the Conservatory, everything was in shambles! Some of the books were still on their sides, hanging off the shelves, but the vast majority of them were lying all over the floor in large, mountainous piles that reached to the ceiling.

"What's going on around here?" Peter asked as his neck strained to see the tops of the piles of books. "This place is a disaster."

He looked around for somebody, but the Conservatory was empty. He put Bobby's LifeBook on a nearby table.

"This is weird," he said. "It's always busy during this time of day."

But it wasn't. No one was removing books from the shelves or climbing the ladders or turning the pages. In fact, Peter didn't see a single person. He ran out of the Conservatory and went over to the Nabi's room. Peter peeked inside and saw the Nabi were still there, but they were just staring forward. They did not move. They just looked frozen. Their quills were on the tables, the ink was in front of them, and empty books sat before them as well, but they did not move.

"What is going on?" Peter yelled and turned in circles, hoping for an answer.

Nobody came to answer his cries. Hoping to get some help, he ran out of the Nabi's room and headed to Miss Penntiworth's office.

"Maybe she can tell me what's going on," he said.

But when Peter turned the corner leading to her office, he ran right into Mr. Grumsby.

"Going somewhere, boy?" Mr. Grumsby snarled.

Peter didn't know what to say.

Mr. Grumsby grabbed the back of Peter's shirt and pulled him down the hall into his office.

"See anything unusual, boy?" he sneered.

Peter looked around and didn't see anything out of the ordinary. That is, nothing out of the ordinary as far as Mr. Grumsby was concerned.

"Unusual?" Peter asked, not in the mood for riddles. "Besides a guy who has thousands of clocks and hourglasses? No, nothing unusual."

Mr. Grumsby grabbed Peter's arm and spun him around towards the stone pedestal where his ancient hourglass sat.

"Take a look at the hourglass, wise guy."

Peter noticed that the sand in the hourglass was moving extremely slow. He could see the grains of sand falling one by one, floating down like snowflakes drifting from the sky. He also noticed the pendulums on the clocks were moving slower, too. They would gradually swing to the side, stay there suspended for a moment or two, and then back to the other side.

"This, boy, is what happens when somebody fools with the books," Mr. Grumsby grunted.

Miss Penntiworth burst into the room. The door slammed against the wall. She turned to Peter, who looked down to the ground.

"Mr. Grumsby, what happened?" she hurriedly asked, her eyes wide and darting between Mr. Grumsby and Peter.

"Perhaps you should ask your protégé," he said as he pointed at Peter. "I told you this wouldn't work. He's not close to being ready."

Peter could barely look at her as she turned around and stared at him.

"Peter, what happened?" she quickly asked.

For a moment, he couldn't speak. He heard the concern in her voice and now felt as though he'd let his only friend down. She walked up to him and put her hand on his shoulder.

"Peter, what happened?" she asked again, softly this time.

Peter sighed. He wasn't sure how to tell her what he'd done, and he felt awful. She was the one true friend he had in this place, and he knew that she'd be crushed by what he was about to tell her. He took a deep breath, sat down, and told her the whole story. He talked about finding Bobby's book and how angry he was, angrier than he'd ever felt in his life. He told her about the dark stranger and how he gave Peter the ink. How he went to the Nabi's room and took the quill. How he wrote in Bobby's book to change the sections he felt were unfair. He then told her how the book had transformed before him. Peter went on and on for what seemed like hours, and once he finished telling his story, he was exhausted. He sat there motionless as Miss Penntiworth stared at him. Peter was waiting for her to yell at him, but she didn't say a word. She just sat down next to him, which made him nervous.

Why doesn't she say something? he thought.

They sat there for a while in complete silence.

"I just have one question," she finally said, breaking the silence. "How do you feel in your heart?"

Peter wasn't sure what she was asking, so he continued to sit there, not exactly sure how to respond.

"Are these the things you truly want to happen to Bobby?" she asked.

She waited for Peter to answer, and for that matter, so was he, but he couldn't say anything. He just sat there. In his mind, he was trying to justify what he'd done. But did he truly want these things to happen to Bobby? He'd thought so, but if it was the right thing to do, why did he feel so awful? Miss Penntiworth touched him on the shoulder.

"If it is not in your heart, then the words you wrote in Bobby's book will not remain. The pages will not be altered. Just as with the Nabi, the words on the page flow from what is inside of them. Your mere temporary anger does not change what is to be," she told him.

Peter was still confused. He wasn't sure what he could say.

"I don't understand," he whispered.

"I know you were temporarily blinded with hate and anger. If you truly have this hate for Bobby, then the ink on those pages will become permanent. You will have succeeded in changing what has been bothering you all this time. You only have to search inside yourself. You have to decide if this is to be Bobby's fate."

Mr. Grumsby was staring at Peter, his visor cocked lower than Peter had ever seen it before. Miss Penntiworth had a look of concern on her face. Peter remembered his mother having that look one time before, when he'd gotten detention at school for writing his own excuse and forging his mother's signature.

What did they want me to do? he asked himself. But he realized that was not the right question to ask. *No,* Peter thought, *this isn't right. What do I want to do?*

He sat there silently for a moment, but then looked up at Miss Penntiworth. "I'm sorry," he said. "This isn't me. I don't want anything bad to happen to anybody."

"You're lying, boy!" Mr. Grumsby said, gritting his teeth as he confronted Peter. "Tell the truth," he snarled.

It only took a second for Peter to answer Mr. Grumsby, and he did so with a tear in his eye. "I am telling the truth," he responded softly.

After he said this, the pendulums on the clocks swung back at their normal speed. Peter looked up at them, and then over to the hourglass. The sand was flowing through the hourglass as it normally did.

Miss Penntiworth looked at him and smiled.

"Of course you don't want to hurt anyone, Peter," she leaned over and hugged him.

He still couldn't look at her. He was so ashamed for what he'd done.

"You know, Peter, maybe you should have taken the time to read more of Bobby's book," she said as she stood up and walked over to Mr. Grumsby's desk.

Picking up the book, she walked up to Peter and handed it to him. Peter was hesitant to take it at first. At this point, he never wanted to see that book again.

"Go ahead, dear, take it," she said.

He reached out and reluctantly took the book, sitting there momentarily staring at the cover. Surprisingly, he wasn't angry any longer. He was actually sad – and not for himself. He was sad for Bobby and the life Bobby faced every day. Peter flipped through a series of pages. Without looking, Miss Penntiworth stopped the pages with her finger.

"Try that one," she said.

Peter looked at the writing on the page, took a breath, and started to read.

"Bobby approached Peter's house. It has been a year since the accident, and Peter's death."

Peter looked around as the mist cleared and found himself in an all too familiar place. He is in his front yard, and everything is as he remembered. The tire swing still hung from the old maple tree, and his bike was leaning up against the side of the garage. Peter reflected on happier times as he stared fondly at his house. His bedroom window was on the second floor, and as he looked up, he noticed his baseball curtains still hanging in the window. He also noticed Bobby out of the corner of his eye.

Bobby had grown some, and Peter watched as he slowly stepped up on to the porch and knocked on the front door. Peter's mother answered the door. Holding a box of tissues, she stood silently as Bobby struggled to look at her. Trying to comfort his mother, Peter reached out for her, but unlike the baby Peter saw earlier, his mother couldn't feel his hand as it brushed past her.

"Yes, can I help you?" she finally said to Bobby, who stood there, unable to speak.

Bobby's mouth opened up for a moment.

"I'm so sorry," he mumbled before he ran away.

Peter raised his head and stared silently at Miss Penntiworth.

"Why don't you take a little time and read some more of the book. Find out how much Bobby's life was fulfilled after you died. I need to talk to Mr. Grumsby for a moment. Here, come out here with me," she said as she led Peter out of Mr. Grumsby's office and sat him down on a wooden bench tucked away in a corner. "You can sit here until I return."

Peter sat on the bench and flipped through a number of other pages. When he got to the part where Bobby won the lottery, he was surprised that he no longer felt anger. He flipped back through some of the previous pages and stopped. As he started to read, Peter found himself standing in a dilapidated old kitchen. The linoleum floor was peeling and cracking, the cabinet doors were barely hanging on, or altogether missing, and a man was sitting at a beat-up metal table with cinder blocks holding up one side. Hearing a door shut behind him, Peter turned around and saw that Bobby had just come home. Bobby glanced quickly at the man, who Peter guesses is Bobby's father. The man is slouched over. In his hand is a beer that he periodically slurps down, and there are eight empty beer cans strewn about. Bobby tried to sneak past his father, but before he got too far, a cold, rough hand grabbed his arm.

"Where have you been?" his father blurted out.

Bobby's mother had seen this all too many times before. She turned back to the stove and continued to cook dinner, fearing what was about to happen.

"I was at baseball practice dad. Remember, I told you–"

CRACK

The force of the slap knocked Bobby's hat onto the floor. He leaned forward and grabbed Bobby's neck with a vice-like grip.

"I thought I told you never to talk back to me. You're more worthless than this one back here," he said, pointing to Bobby's mother.

Bobby noticed that his mother did not move. Still holding onto Bobby's neck, he threw him to the ground.

"Pick up that hat and get out of my sight, you piece of dirt," he grumbled through a beer-soaked slur.

Bobby lay still on the floor, tasting something only too familiar to him as a trickle of blood flowed from his lower lip. Peter watched as Bobby stood up and took a deep breath. This is a totally different person than what Peter was used to seeing. Here, Bobby was as submissive as a newborn puppy. His face was stinging from the force of the slap, but he didn't say a word as he picked up his hat and put it on his head. Staring at him through squinty eyes, his father chuckled as he took another swig of beer.

"You can wear that hat all you want, you'll never amount to anything, let alone a ballplayer," he told Bobby with a snicker.

Bobby tried to hold it back, but he couldn't any longer, and he started to cry. This enraged his father.

"What are you doing, crying?" he screamed at Bobby.

His father staggered up off his chair and onto his feet.

"You piece of dirt, get out of here before I bash your brains in!" he said as he stumbled after Bobby and took a swing at him.

Bobby ran down the hall to his room.

"And no dinner tonight, you crybaby! You'll eat when you learn to be a man!" his father yelled.

Bobby went into his room and forced his door shut. It barely worked any longer after all of the years his father tried to kick it down. Just to make sure, Bobby pushed his dresser up against it. This usually worked to keep his father out. By the time he had finished his beer, he was too drunk to put a great effort in getting to Bobby anyway. Bobby wiped his tears with his tattered sleeve and walked over to his window. Peter took a moment to look around. Bobby's room was far different than Peter's. There were no toys on the shelves, no pictures on the walls. There wasn't even a set of sheets on the bed, or at least what Bobby used for a bed, which was an old, worn out mattress that lay on the floor. On top of that was a raggedy old blanket and a stained pillow. Peter walked up behind Bobby, who was still looking out the window and sniffling.

"What did I do to deserve a life like this?" Bobby whispered as he grabbed his stomach.

It ached from hunger, but that was normal because he was rarely allowed to eat dinner.

"I didn't ask for this."

Looking out the window, he knew there was more to life than what he had now. He knew somewhere out there was happiness for him.

As Peter flipped through some more of the pages, he found himself back in the retro diner with his family. It was raining outside, and he watched Bobby sitting on his bike in the cold, hiding under the remnants of a cardboard box he was using as an umbrella. His father had just kicked him out of the house, and Bobby knew that the restaurant usually threw out some decent food. As Bobby sat there waiting for his meal, he watched the shadowed presence of Peter sitting inside with his parents, laughing and joking. He saw Peter's father reach across the table and rub Peter's head just before his mother gave him a hug. Bobby started to cry as the rain beat down on him. He'd never experienced that type of love. Just before Bobby pedaled away from the restaurant, he looked back at Peter's family once more. Bobby grunted in disgust as he watched them share a super-sized ice cream sundae.

Peter turned a few pages forward. He is now in a dugout at his old baseball field. He looked over at Bobby, who is sitting on the corner of the bench by himself. The baseball game had just finished, and everyone is leaving. Bobby stared at Peter's former self who is running up to his father. Peter's father picked him up and spun him around. Bobby continued to sit there, punching his fist into his glove as he watched all of his teammates smiling with their families. Again, he turned to Peter and watched as his father hugged him. This made Bobby sneer, and he spit on the floor in disgust. There's no father to rub his head, no family to congratulate him for a good game, nobody there to pick him up and spin him around. As the last car left the parking lot, Bobby got up from the bench, climbed onto his bike, and pedaled home slowly, hoping his father would be asleep by now, or at least too drunk to realize he's home.

Peter flipped through another few pages, and upon reading the section he settled on, he found himself at the scene of his accident. Beyond the delivery truck, now resting on the sidewalk, Peter sees Bobby shaking with fear as he jumps up, gets onto his bike, and quickly pedals away. Bobby's heart is pounding, and he can't seem to catch his breath.

"Peter's alright," he says. "He has to be alright. He just fell over. The truck never hit him. Please let him be ok. I will never bother him again, I swear, please."

Bobby skidded to a stop around the corner and looked back. The truck driver and several other people who have stopped their cars are now standing over Peter's lifeless body. One woman looked and screamed. Peter watched her as she backs away, crying uncontrollably.

"Call 9-1-1!" somebody yelled.

Bobby too starts to cry as he hears sirens approaching in the background. The mist encompasses Peter, and he finds himself in the town's cemetery.

It's the morning of Peter's funeral, and Bobby is there. It doesn't look like he's slept in days, and he's still wearing his baseball uniform from the day of the accident. Bobby slowly pedaled his bike through the iron gates at the entrance of the cemetery, and past row upon row of headstones. In the distance, there's a line of cars parked under the shade of several maple trees. Bobby stopped just before the crowd of people, and leaned his bike up against an old stone mausoleum; the granite of the structure is cracked and covered with moss and mold. Peter watched as Bobby took off his baseball cap and peeked around the corner.

A large crowd is gathered at the gravesite, but this doesn't surprise Bobby. He knew Peter was a good kid. He recognized that most of the kids from school are there. Just to the side of the grave, Bobby sees Peter's mother and father sitting under a white tent behind a small brown coffin covered with flowers. They're both dressed in black, and his mother is holding Peter's baseball cap. Everything around them is pristine. The chairs are evenly spaced on either side of the tent, and the coffin is so polished that it reflects the numerous flower arrangements. Even the dirt mound, which would later cover young Peter, is hidden under a smoothed out green carpet.

Bobby watched Peter's parents, staring straight ahead and crying as the priest spoke. He couldn't hear the words, but nonetheless, he started to cry. Peter's parents looked as though all of the life was gone from their eyes. Somehow, Bobby knew exactly how they were feeling. While the priest spoke, Bobby had time to reflect back. He realized that he never truly had anything against Peter and that he definitely never wanted anything like this to happen to him. All of the rage he'd felt for Peter was out of jealousy for what Peter had, especially the family that Bobby wished he had. From the father who cared enough to show up to his baseball games, to the mother who loved him enough to protect him against anything. This is what Bobby craved. Bobby fell to his knees with his hand pressed up against the cold stone of the mausoleum that hid him from the crowd of people. He was crying so hard now that he made himself sick.

He couldn't look any longer. Instead, he kneeled on the ground among the thickets and weeds growing up around him, sobbing uncontrollably. Emotions poured out of him as the flood gates in his eyes continued to cascade tears down his cheeks. It was just starting to get dark when he looked up and saw the last car leaving the gravesite. The sun disappeared behind the rows of stone markers as the shadows slowly crept toward him. Although exhausted from his outpouring of emotions, Bobby stood up and walked near the freshly covered grave. It had been hours since the mourners had departed. Bobby's whole body trembled as he approached the grave. He stared down at the gray stone marker, framed with two angels holding a banner with Peter's name on it. Bobby read the inscription.

Here Lies Peter, The Best Son A Family Could Hope For. He Was Loved As Much As Anyone Can Be Loved And Will Be Greatly Missed.

Bobby dropped to the ground.

"I never really knew you," he choked through his tears. "I never hated you…I am so sorry… I would give anything to take this back."

Bobby curled up in a ball next to the marker, his insides erupting, and he shook so much that he hurt. He lay there for several moments before getting up to leave, and as he left, he placed his baseball cap on Peter's headstone before backing away. He was exhausted, and not sure what he could do or say.

Peter was now sitting back on his bench, not believing what he had just read. He now realized that Bobby didn't hate him; he hated himself.

Peter looked back at the book and continued to read. He was now standing in the middle of a lobby inside an office building. Looking over, Peter thought he recognized someone who looked like Bobby, although he was much older now. This surprised him because Bobby was no longer in ratty, old clothes like the ones he wore in the alley. He was now dressed in a dark suit and tie, clean-shaven, with his hair graying and cut short. Across from Bobby was a man handing him a stack of papers, which he set down on a table and signed.

"Congratulations, Mr. Crones. That should take care of everything," the man told him.

Bobby just nodded at the man and walked out of the lobby. Something unusual happens that Peter never experienced before. The words, which are written in Bobby's book, not only echo out, they are projected in front of him in bold-gold lettering.

"Robert Crones takes most of the lottery winnings and starts a foundation for battered and abused children."

Peter finds himself in an all too familiar haze. He is now standing on a sidewalk in front of a four-story brick building. Peter looked up at the entry and noticed a name on the placard.

"Peter's Home. A Safe Place for Battered and Abused Children."

"He named the foundation after me?" Peter asked.

Peter climbed the steps and entered the foyer. In the entrance of the foundation, there is nothing more than a large oil painting hanging majestically on the nearby wall. As Peter approached it, he sees a recreation of himself from his little league baseball card picture. It seems so long ago, him smiling in his yellow and white uniform, holding a baseball bat on his shoulder. Below the portrait is a brass nameplate that simply reads, "Peter". He watched Bobby standing silently in front of the portrait, staring at it like he does every day.

"Mr. Crones?" a young man interrupts.

Bobby breaks out of his trance and looks at the young clerk.

"Yes."

"I've been meaning to ask you, who is Peter?"

Bobby hesitated for a moment, reflecting on an image etched in his memory for many years.

"Peter is a person who died because he was treated like he didn't matter," he said as he turned away from the clerk and continued to stare at the portrait.

As the clerk walked away, Peter sees Bobby's eyes glisten.

"I hope you can one day forgive me, Peter, because I will never forgive myself," he tells the portrait before he turns and walks away, his head staring at the ground.

"There is no denying this boy did terrible things to you, Peter," Miss Penntiworth said, startling Peter who hadn't noticed her standing next to him in the foyer.

She was also staring at Peter's painting.

"But when you look at it, you changed his life. He became a great man because of you, and more than that, his foundation, your foundation, helps hundreds of children every year. Children who might not have otherwise had a chance at life. If it weren't for you, none of this would be possible. Yes, you died. But by you dying, so many have lived. Is that fair? Maybe not to you, or to your parents, but I could only wish my death helped a fraction of the people that have been helped by you dying."

Peter was speechless. The mist formed again, and he was back, sitting on the bench next to Miss Penntiworth. He still didn't know what to say as he looked at the book, then at Miss Penntiworth. After giving her a slight smile, he stood up and handed her Bobby's book before walking down the hall to his room.

CHAPTER 18
His End is Near

Peter walked slowly back to his room. As he reflected upon everything that had just happened, he felt ashamed for what he had done, and he wasn't sure what consequences he would face for causing so much trouble. Thinking back to the times when he was home and would get into trouble, he couldn't remember an instance that even came close to what he'd done today. As odd as it seemed, this caused him to long for home once again. He would give anything to be back there, waiting for his father to get home and hand out his punishment. As Peter reached his room, he wasn't tired. He had lots to think about, so he walked through his section before he went to bed.

As soon as Peter opened the door, he noticed everything returned back to the way it was. Yet something caused Peter to feel uneasy. He couldn't put his finger on it, but the room did not have the same familiar feeling, which left him unsettled. Immediately he walked over to the tapestry. It had been pulled to the side, and he noticed that the mysterious door was now there, and it was open! Peter ran out of the room and down the hall to Mr. Grumsby's office, where he and Miss Penntiworth were drinking a cup of tea and talking.

"The door is there again!" Peter yelled as he burst into the room.

Mr. Grumsby spit out his tea, again startled by Peter's entrance.

"Where, boy?" he sputtered.

Peter pointed down the hall.

"In my section, straight through, against the far wall where it was last time."

Mr. Grumsby grabbed the hourglass, and he, Peter, and Miss Penntiworth scrambled down the hall to Peter's section. They cautiously entered Section III and noticed the door that Peter found open was still there. As they inched their way closer, Mr. Grumsby stuck his arm out and stopped Peter. He looked at the hourglass and then at Peter.

"I guess I have no choice but to trust you with this," he grumbled as he handed Peter the hourglass. "Maybe you can redeem yourself and not screw this up."

Peter just frowned at him. Even though he didn't like being treated that way, Mr. Grumsby was right to say what he did.

"Like I told you before, if there is any trouble, tilt the hourglass to the side. Make sure no sand is flowing. Understand?" he instructed Peter.

Peter nodded, and Mr. Grumsby turned to the door, walked up to it, and slowly pushed it open further. The hinges creaked, and he and Miss Penntiworth carefully entered into the darkness beyond. The torches did not pop to life as they had for Peter. Miss Penntiworth looked back at Peter and gave him a reassuring look.

"It will be all right, dear," she said before disappearing into the darkness.

It seemed like hours passed by as Peter waited, crouched up against one of the bookshelves. Suddenly, the door slammed shut, and he heard a scream. He ran to the door and tried to open it, but it was locked. Frantic, Peter pulled on the handle and then started to kick it.

"Miss Penntiworth!" he screamed. "Mr. Grumsby, what's happening?"

Peter kept pulling on the door latch, and when that didn't work, he scrambled around the room looking for something to ram the door with. Then, after he remembered what Mr. Grumsby had told him, he quickly tilted the hourglass on its side. As soon as he did, everything in the room changed. He looked out one of the windows and noticed a bird had frozen in mid-flight. Even the particles of dust in the room remained suspended in the air. Peter held the hourglass up close to his eyes and examined it, making certain none of the grains of sand were flowing into the other chamber. Sure enough, the sand lay still in its respective bulbs.

"What in tarnation happened here?"

Peter quickly recognized Charlie's voice.

"Charlie! They're trapped in there! I can't get them out!"

Charlie hobbled up to the door and pulled on the latch. It didn't budge.

"Dang it!" he muttered, looking around. "Wait, I got it! Follow me Slick."

Peter followed Charlie down the corridor towards an open door.

"Let's go in here," he said.

"Charlie, what happened? What are we going to do? Where are Mr. Grumsby and Miss Penntiworth?" Peter asked, gasping for breath.

"Not to worry, Slick," he told him. "Just make sure you have the hourglass, and follow me."

They walked over to a tapestry that showed two wolves snarling at each other embroidered on it.

"We'll be safe down here," he said with a faint smile at the corner of his lips.

Charlie pulled the tapestry aside, revealing a tall wooden door. As he pushed it open, it creaked loudly. Torches lining a staircase leading downward burst into flames and illuminated the path.

"This way, Slick," he said.

Peter looked down and noticed the sands of the hourglass were still not moving. Just as he stepped onto the first step of the staircase, he paused.

"Charlie," he said quietly, cautiously.

Charlie stopped suddenly from his descent down the staircase. "Yes, Peter," he whispered to him without turning around.

"How are you able to move?" he asked.

He still refused to look at him.

"What do you mean?"

"The hourglass," Peter said. "The sand is stopped. I thought only the holder of the hourglass and Mr. Grumsby were able to move when the sand is standing still?"

There was a moment's hesitation before Charlie answered.

"Well that's really simple, Slick," he said before suddenly turning around and lurching at him. "Give me that glass, boy!" he snarled with a voice that echoed with evil. Charlie's eyes were now yellowed over with flames flickering in his pupils.

"No!" Peter jumped and then backed away from the tapestry.

As Charlie melted from the shadows, his face changed into a disfigured mass. Where there were once warm, friendly eyes had now turned into sunken yellowish-green specks set deep into a patch of scaly skin, barely anything more than a simple covering for the vein-ridden skull that lay beneath.

"It's you!" Peter cried. "It can't be! Charlie, please, no…"

"Yes, Peter, it is I," Apius said as he replaced the hood upon his head. "Probably your only friend left after the stunt you pulled with that book," he sneered.

"The stunt I pulled? You're the one who gave me the ink!" Peter yelled, still walking backward.

"Yes, yes, I did, Peter, but I didn't provide you with the quill, did I? I didn't hide the book in that pillowcase, did I? And I did not force your hand to open the jar and etch those words, did I now, Peter?" Apius asked as he walked toward Peter.

He hated to admit it, but Apius was right.

"However, as you correctly stated, Peter, I did indeed give you the ink," Apius said. "And now in return, I need that hourglass."

Peter kept walking backward, looking for a chance to run. Apius smiled at him.

"It's only fair. I gave you something you sought, now you can give me what I seek," he said as his bony finger pointed to the hourglass.

Peter wouldn't stop, and now Apius's voice became more forceful.

"I have sought and yearned for the power of that hourglass for centuries now. Waiting for the right moment, for the right person to come along and help me get it. Now is that time, Peter, and you are that person."

Peter's hand reached behind him, hoping to find a door.

"Why are you standing in this cold, dark room when you could be home with your family?" Apius asked him. "Once I have possession of that hourglass, I can make that happen for you."

This caused Peter to stop, and as he stood there staring at Apius, Apius's face creaked out a little smile.

"Yes, boy, your family," he said to Peter. "You remember them, don't you? Wouldn't you like to be having dinner with them instead of watching them eat all alone in that diner you favor so much? Or have you stopped caring for them already? You have hardly been here long enough to already brush them aside like crumbs on a plate."

Peter just stared at Apius, unable to say anything.

"Your mother is probably worried about you," said Apius. "How many times a day do you think she begs for your return?"

With that, Apius's figure turned into one that was all too familiar to Peter. His mother was standing there, looking sad as she reached out to him.

"And what of your father?" Apius said, his voice now that of Peter's mother.

Peter snapped out of his trance only to drift into another. He saw his father standing there before him smiling and throwing a baseball into a glove.

"Don't you want to play catch, Peter?" Apius asked, his voice again morphing until it matched that of his father.

"You're the one who left that book about the diners for me to find," Peter whispered. "And the photo of my parents. You're the one who brought it to the library. But why?" he asked.

"I didn't want you to forget them," Apius said. "After how sad you seemed, I just wanted to help you see them again, so I found them for you," he told Peter. "Hand me the hourglass, and you can be with them again for good."

Apius held his hand out for Peter, who now gradually started to walk closer to Apius. As though he was in a trance, Peter slowly handed Apius the hourglass, but suddenly stopped, glanced at the hourglass, then at Apius. He remembered how Apius had tried to fool him before. He also remembered the trust he felt with Miss Penntiworth, and the fear he felt with Apius. All of this caused him to stop.

"You're lying!" he screamed. "You don't care if I ever get home, or if I ever get back together with my parents!"

With a quick wave of his hand, Apius caused all of the shutters in the room to slam shut, casting the room into an eerie darkness. Peter immediately scrambled to reach one of the doors.

"No!" Apius screamed, thrusting his hand to Peter's direction, and forcing the doors to slam shut as well.

Peter didn't know what to do. There was no other way out.

"Now, Peter, let's not make this difficult. Trust me, you do not want to make this difficult," he sneered as he moved closer. "With that hourglass, I can right some wrongs of my own. The intolerableness of that world you come from; the maniacal way this place is run. Yes, I too shall right a few wrongs."

Apius continued to come at Peter.

"If you had the strength I initially gave you credit for, you too could have made some changes. You could have joined me and corrected the flaws, the misgivings all around us."

Just as Apius drew closer, Peter made a quick dash away from him in hopes of somehow escaping. He didn't make it far. Apius cast a ring of fire around him, trapping him. Peter turned in circles, looking for a way to flee, and within the flames, he saw reflections of Bobby and his friends as they picked on Peter, tormenting him. All of Peter's miseries were projected before him as Apius slowly walked through the fire. The flames flickered in his eyes as he drew closer. His long, pointed fingers reached for the hourglass as Peter backed away. Soon he began to feel the heat on his back, and he knew he was coming close to the edge of the circle.

"That's it, boy. Your end is near," Apius snarled. "Give me the hourglass, and I will make it peaceful for you. Cross me, and you will suffer a thousand deaths."

As Apius approached Peter, he smiled. There was nowhere to go. Apius grabbed him by the shirt collar and effortlessly raised him off the ground. He stared straight into Peter's eyes as Peter kicked his legs frantically in an effort to escape.

"Let's just finish this, shall we?" Apius sneered as he changed hands and held Peter by the neck.

Apius's fingers burned like branding irons resting on Peter's neck, his skin searing from the grasp. Apius laughed at the sound of the sizzling skin and tightened his grip.

"Ahhh!" Peter screamed from the pain.

"Let go of the hourglass, Peter, and this shall be quick," Apius said.

Peter was barely able to gasp. His clothes were starting to fray and tatter. His skin turned gray and wrinkled as the years of his youth were being drawn out of him.

"Never," he choked out as his lifeforce was quickly being consumed by Apius.

Just as everything turned blurry, Peter heard a familiar voice.

"How long you been after that dusty old thing, Apius?" the voice said, coming from the corner of the room.

The flames around Peter immediately died out as Apius dropped him to the ground and turned.

"What are you doing here, old man?" Apius asked.

"Hmph. Shouldn't you be answering that question?" said the voice Peter now recognized.

He slowly looked over and saw Mr. Grumsby sitting in a chair in the corner of the room, whittling a piece of wood into what appeared to be a puppy.

"It's too late," Apius said, pointing over to the clump of clothing that was Peter. "The boy is mine."

Barely conscious, his skin returned to normal, Peter raised his head as he tried to warn Mr. Grumsby.

"Run…" was all Peter could whisper, using the last bit of energy he had to tuck the hourglass underneath him in a feeble attempt to hide it.

Mr. Grumsby's visor bent up as he saw this, and went back to whittling his piece of wood. "Too late, Apius?" he said without even looking up. "Now, you sure about that? I think you're losing your touch. This boy doesn't have any evil in him. Why you wasting our time here?"

"No evil here, eh?" asked Apius as he cautiously approached Mr. Grumsby. "Your mind is growing weak, old man. You remember in the past when changing one of these LifeBooks was considered evil?"

"Nah. Not this time," said Mr. Grumsby. "I see it more as a young boy's curiosity. You might call it being mischievous, but not evil, no."

Mr. Grumsby stood, which caused Apius to immediately step backward toward Peter. Peter watched Apius's hand slowly reach back. He knew Apius was going to try to grab the hourglass, but all Mr. Grumsby did was blow the wood shavings off his statue and rub his hand over it.

"You should try spending your time doing this, Apius. It relaxes you," he said.

Apius didn't say a word. He just kept reaching for the hourglass, slowly, cautiously.

"Now, I wouldn't do that," Mr. Grumsby said sternly.

Apius stopped. "What do you mean old man?" Apius said, smiling sinisterly at Mr. Grumsby.

"You know exactly what I mean," Mr. Grumsby said as he folded his pocketknife and put it into his pocket. "I'm growing tired of this."

Mr. Grumsby's visor was bent to a perfect V shape above his eyes as he scowled at Apius and walked forward.

"There is no evil in this room for you to feed off. I believe that puts me with the advantage," Mr. Grumsby told him. "Now why don't you be a good little creature of the dark and get on out of here before we all have a bad day?"

Nobody did anything for what seemed like several minutes. Mr. Grumsby calmly stood there, never taking his eyes off of Apius, and Apius looked back and forth between Mr. Grumsby and Peter. Then in a flash, Apius gnashed his yellow teeth together, turned to Peter, and lurched forward. Peter huddled down on the ground but was instantly turned over with a flick of Apius's hand.

"Arrghh!" Apius screamed.

"Looking for this?" Mr. Grumsby asked, causing Apius to stop as he held his hand over Peter.

Apius quickly spun around to see what Mr. Grumsby was talking about. As he turned, a hot wind rushed over Peter, who looked at Mr. Grumsby, and saw he was now holding the hourglass. Peter was astonished. Just a minute ago, the hourglass had been tucked beneath him. He was sure he'd had the tightest grip possible on the hourglass.

"I think its time for you to go, Apius," Mr. Grumsby said, smiling while Apius just stood there, frozen, unsure what to do next.

"Not before I take the boy with me!" cried Apius as he lunged back at Peter.

Peter scrambled for something to protect himself with. Reaching his hand into his pocket, his fingers brushed the feathery softness of the quill. He quickly pulled it out and pointed the sharpened tip at Apius. Immediately Peter's hand felt the moist, tattered rags of Apius's cloak as the quill sunk into his skin beneath. Apius howled in agony as the quill began to draw in the years of stolen ink from his wretched body. Black ink coursed through his veins and pooled around the tip of the quill as it reclaimed past stolen lives. Apius's eyes began to once again glaze over. He mustered up enough strength to stumble backward and pull the quill from his body, staring at it before throwing it across the room.

"You will pay for this you worthless sack of meat!" Apius coughed out as he collapsed onto the ground.

"Not today, he won't." Mr. Grumsby exclaimed as he shook the hourglass up and down.

A brilliant white light flowed from the hourglass and washed throughout the room. Unable to see anything, Peter covered his eyes with his arm, and through the light, he heard Apius scream, then everything fell silent. When the light from the room diminished, Peter lifted his head and looked around. He was still lying on the floor, but Apius and Mr. Grumsby were nowhere to be seen. Peter tried to move, but he was so exhausted, he fell into a deep sleep.

CHAPTER 19
A New Chapter

When Peter woke up, he was lying on Miss Penntiworth's couch under one of her thick comforters. The fire warming the room flickered and crackled in the fireplace. He finally felt at ease, which was quite a difference from what he'd felt only a few hours ago. The clock softly chimed on the wall as Miss Penntiworth sat down next to him. Peter looked over and saw Mr. Grumsby sitting in a rocking chair by the fire, still whittling his piece of wood.

"What happened?" Peter asked as he felt the bruises on his neck.

Miss Penntiworth pulled the comforter back and helped him sit up.

"Well, to put it quite simply, Peter, you triumphed over evil. Just like I always knew you would."

This didn't seem to concern Peter at the moment.

"What about the hourglass? Is it safe?" he asked, looking around the room for it.

"Don't worry, Peter. It is perfectly safe," Miss Penntiworth said, giving him a reassuring smile.

"I never did care for that Apius guy," Mr. Grumsby said from the corner of the room as he continued carving his wood. "He always gave me the willies. But I'm surprised he came after you Peter. I may have underestimated you. You're one of the strongest people I've met in a long time, and trust me, I've seen them come and go."

Peter rubbed the back of his head as he tried to figure this out. This was the first time Mr. Grumsby had called him by his name.

Was I dreaming all of this?

Mr. Grumsby stopped carving the figurine, and his visor tilted up.

"No. It really happened," he said. "Here, why don't you keep this?" He stood up and tossed the now painted statue of the puppy to Peter.

"Nice catch, kid." Mr. Grumsby told him. "I bet you were a heck of a ballplayer."

Mr. Grumsby stretched his arms into the air, yawned and as he walked away, he stopped for a moment and checked the time on his pocket watch.

"Well, time to go. There's a new fishing spot I want to try, and I don't like to be late," said Mr. Grumsby. "You take good care of him, Miss Penntiworth."

She put her arm around Peter and helped him up off the couch.

"Let's get you to bed, dear," she said as she wrapped the comforter around him. "Tomorrow starts a new chapter in your life."

As they walked to his room, Peter felt better. Now that he was thinking more clearly, his head filled with questions, so he figured he would try to get some answers from Miss Penntiworth, or else he'd never get to sleep.

"Miss Penntiworth, how was Apius able to move around? I had the hourglass tipped onto its side, so none of the sand was moving. I thought nobody was supposed to be able to move besides me? *I am* the one who held the hourglass, not Apius," he said.

"You see, Peter, there was still evil lingering in you from when you made the changes to Robert's book, and as long as there is evil present for Apius to feed off, he is able to present himself and move around freely," she explained. "Since he was feeding off the little evil inside you, and you were able to move, so was Apius."

"How could he hurt me? I am already, well, you know," he said.

"You're correct, Peter, Apius could not really hurt you physically," Miss Penntiworth told him. "However, it was your soul he was interested in. He can destroy and consume the soul of a person. If he destroys the soul, it will never move forward. It perishes, disappears. Then Apius absorbs it, and he grows stronger because of it."

When they got to Peter's room, Miss Penntiworth opened the door and walked Peter over to his bed.

"Miss Penntiworth, how did–"

"I think that's enough questions for tonight, Peter. We can pick up where we left off tomorrow. I think some rest is in order for you," she said as she fluffed his pillow.

Peter started to say something, but a yawn interrupted him. "I am tired," he said, letting out another big yawn.

"You get a good night's rest, dear," Miss Penntiworth said. "We have a big day ahead of us tomorrow."

"What are we doing?" he asked her in a sleepy haze.

"Peter, my dear, tomorrow starts a new chapter for you," she whispered as she walked out of the room.

CHAPTER 20
A Simple Throne

After what happened the day before, Peter was happy to find himself in his room. Just outside, sunlight shimmered off the waves of the ocean, and the reflection danced across his ceiling. He walked over to the window and watched the rhythmic rolling of the waves as a pod of dolphins jumped in and out of the surf. This had become one of Peter's favorite scenes.

There was a soft knock at the door, and when Peter turned around, he saw Miss Penntiworth standing in his room. After his encounter with Apius, Peter was apprehensive, but it only took a moment before he felt the warmth of her smile and knew it could only come from the real Miss Penntiworth. In her hands was a tray of waffles smothered in strawberries and whipped cream.

"Would you mind if I joined you for breakfast, Peter?" she asked as she set the tray down on the desk.

"I would like that," he said to her.

Peter brought two chairs over and set them down next to the window. Miss Penntiworth and Peter then moved his desk over to the window to use as a table. They sat down for the better part of an hour eating their waffles and looking out the window. It was quiet and peaceful, and they hardly said a word to each other. Every now and then they'd look at each other and smile, and when the last waffle had been eaten, Peter sat back and rubbed his stomach.

"I can't remember ever eating that many waffles before," he said.

Miss Penntiworth smiled at him. "They were quite excellent," she said, dabbing the side of her mouth with a white linen napkin.

Peter felt she was acting a little differently, but after yesterday's excitement, he thought that everybody would be a little different today. Miss Penntiworth looked at Peter, but then she turned away. There was an awkward moment of silence that he found odd until she finally sighed.

"Why don't we take a walk, Peter?" she said as she stood up, folded her napkin, and placed it on the table.

"Um, sure," he said.

When he walked over to grab his sneakers, Peter saw the picture of his parents sitting on the nightstand. He picked up the picture, put it in his back pocket, and smiled at Miss Penntiworth. After he finished tying his shoes, he followed her into the hallway. He wasn't sure why, but he turned around and looked at his room before they walked out. It stayed quiet for several minutes, but Peter's curiosity got the best of him.

"Miss Penntiworth, who is Apius?" he asked.

"Well, Peter, it's hard to explain, but the short answer is that Apius is pure evil in human form."

Peter waited for more of an answer, but it was apparent that he wasn't getting one unless he asked.

"What does Apius do? I mean, you know, what makes him so bad?" he asked.

"Well, for one thing, he seeks out LifeBooks on the shelves and takes them away," she said. "They are not his to take."

"Yeah, but I've never heard of any books going missing before. Wouldn't he be able to go into the Conservatory and clear off a bunch of shelves before anyone could find him?" he asked, somewhat confused.

"It's not that simple," she told him. "You see, he has to seek out the ones where people have strayed from the path of good and righteousness, and he has to find them at the precise time they stray if he has any hope of converting them. Once he finds those people, he takes the books away with him so he can stop the person before they have a chance to redeem themselves. Take Robert's book, for instance, he could have kept the book and kept Robert in his most unpleasant form, but Apius got greedy. He felt by giving you the book, you would make sure Robert never redeemed himself, and then he would have you, too. You, Peter, were headed down the path of evil by making those changes. Fortunately, you are such a good person that you were able to stop yourself before you went too far."

Peter was surprised by what she'd said.

"I don't feel like such a good person," he told her.

"Oh, but you are, Peter," she reassured him. "You are one of the most special people that I have run across, and I have come across some great people."

There were several moments of silence before Peter asked Miss Penntiworth some more questions. He wasn't sure how much he could ask, or how much he was allowed to know, but he didn't see the harm of asking until she stopped answering.

"If I'm so good and nice, why did Apius come after me?" he asked.

"Well, Peter, as I explained, he got greedy. He wasn't happy just trying to take Robert. He wanted you because he saw how honest and pure you were. He must have felt it would be a great triumph to turn you away from good," she told him. "Plus, he apparently saw you as a way to the hourglass."

Peter got quiet for a moment, stopped, and looked at Miss Penntiworth, his eyes glistening. "Apius promised, if I helped him, he'd let me return home to my parents," Peter said softly.

Miss Penntiworth hugged Peter. She then held onto both of his shoulders and looked him directly in his eyes. "Nobody has the power to do that, Peter. If I could have, I would have sent you home to your parents a long time ago," she said, hesitating for a moment. "And you know Mr. Grumsby would have been more than happy to send you home."

She winked at him, which caused Peter to smile.

"Apius would have told you anything, dear, to get that hourglass," she said to him. "I know how much you miss your parents and how much they miss you, but I'm sorry Peter. I can assure you that neither Apius, Mr. Grumsby, nor I have that power."

Peter believed what she said. As odd as it seemed, he felt some comfort knowing that nobody, including Apius, could have helped him get home. Even though helping Apius was something Peter now knew he could never do, he was glad he hadn't missed the chance to go home.

"Who exactly is, or was, Apius?" he asked.

"Well, Apius was a Nabi that found a way out of his penance."

Peter was shocked.

"He was a Nabi?"

"Yes, he was," she told him. "He worked here many, many years ago. When he first arrived, he was no different than any of the other Nabi around him. Then, as time went on, people noticed something unusual. Most of the books Apius scrolled turned out to be ones where the person succumbed to evil. Nobody thought much of it at first; that was just the way things were supposed to be. However, Apius seemed to thrive on the evil he wrote. He began to scroll more and more books where the person became evil. Other things about him changed as well."

"Like what?" Peter asked.

"Well, if you spend enough time with the Nabi, you will hear them wail in pain. It's rare, but it happens occasionally. The wailing comes from the guilt they feel for what they have done. Apius, however, was different. Apius never wailed. The only noise you would hear coming from him was laughter, something that you never hear the Nabi do. Every once in a while, you would hear him laugh a low, deep, raspy laugh. It was as though he got pleasure from the evil he had written. That's why when he touches a book, he absorbs the person in the book."

"I think I saw that when he picked up Bobby's book," Peter said. "It frayed and fell apart and stuff."

"That's how it happens, Peter. He needs evil to continue living, so that's why he seeks it out," she explained.

"How was he able to get away, from being a Nabi?"

"Well, long ago, it used to be that the Nabi handled their own books from start to finish. They would get the new books, get their own ink, write about the person, and then return the books to the carts. When Apius retrieved his ink, he had a knack for picking out the evil ones. He would stand in front of the shelf where the jars are kept and just stare at them. We would watch him standing there for a long time, then all of a sudden, he would reach forward and snatch an ink jar off the shelf. He instinctively knew which jar to pick. The more evil the person would be, the happier it made Apius. After a while, he wouldn't write in the books any longer. He actually began to consume the ink."

"What do you mean he consumed the ink?" Peter asked.

"Well, he drank it," she told Peter matter-of-factly. "To consume the ink is a mortal sin. There is no coming back from that. By doing so, you are stealing people's lives. But for Apius, it made him change; it made him grow, and by consuming the ink, he grew stronger. Once he took his first sip, he began to crave the ink. Before long, just drinking the ink wasn't enough for him. It was then that he started going into the sections of the Conservatory and seeking out the books of persons that were evil. When those became harder to find, he looked for the LifeBooks of people that were merely headed down the wrong path. Once he found those, he would then absorb them before they had a chance to redeem themselves. Once we found out what he was up to, it was too late. He had become too strong. He had found power and magic from the ink he consumed, and from that point, Apius disappeared. Searches were conducted, and to this day, as you witnessed, we are still looking for him. Back here, things had to change. It was decided no Nabi could be allowed to handle the whole process. Now, as you know, different people handle different jobs, and the Nabi only write the words. It has been that way now for centuries. Fortunately, there are not many people like Apius around. We keep watch on the Nabi in case one of them shows themselves to be evil."

"Have any of the Nabi turned evil since then?" Peter asked.

"Oh, thank goodness, no," Miss Penntiworth told him.

"But what about yesterday?" he asked. "He was right there. Why didn't anyone get rid of Apius then?"

"That raises an interesting question, Peter. I'm not exactly sure, but it makes me wonder what would happen if Apius is ever destroyed. First of all, would evil end? If it did, could good exist without evil?"

Peter's head tilted to the side, and he furrowed his brow.

"Wouldn't it be awesome if everybody was good?" he asked, thinking the answer was obvious.

"Maybe so, dear, but if evil did not exist, would we be able to comprehend what is good and what is not good?" she asked him. "Just think about it, Peter. If there was nothing but good in the world, would we start to question what is truly good? If there were no evil, only good, how would we know when something is better than something else? When does good become evil? If that boy is good because he has straight A's in school, does that mean a boy with B's is bad? What if another boy has straight A's *and* he helps his mother out at home. Does that make the other boy with straight A's less good? He's good, but maybe not as good as the other boy. Maybe the presence of bad or evil, allows us to gauge what is good."

At first, Peter thought the answer was obvious. Now in talking with Miss Penntiworth, maybe the answer wasn't so clear. He thought for a moment.

"Why did Apius want the hourglass so badly?" he asked as they continued to walk.

"Well, Peter, if Apius were to get his hands on the hourglass, it would enable him to live forever," she told him. "However, that is not the worse part. If Apius had the hourglass, life as we know it would cease to exist."

"The hourglass is powerful enough to destroy everything?" Peter asked.

"No, not exactly," she said. "Since Apius has to survive by absorbing evil, having the hourglass would allow him to stop time. In doing so, he would have, well, basically eternity to scour through the Conservatory, unimpeded, and search each book looking for evil. When that wasn't an option any longer, or he grew tired of searching, he could then take, well someone like yourself, who is at a crossroads in their life, and manipulate them to do something wrong. If the person did not do something evil, then Apius could return to a point in time, and try to further manipulate that person into doing something evil. In essence, Peter, Apius could control every LifeBook in the library."

"What happens to the people in the books Apius takes?" Peter asked.

"They either pass on by some means, or they walk through life as soulless creatures. You may have heard about or seen them before. They are the people who do not care about anybody or anything. They are the people your parents see in the local news or read about in newspapers. For the most part, it is an unfortunate circumstance for them. Most people, when they take a wrong turn in life, correct themselves at one time or another. It's human nature to want to be good. Unfortunately, sometimes Apius removes that chance at redemption. Take Robert, for instance. His life was headed down the path of darkness. Apius already had his book. He could have kept the book, and Robert's life would have been frozen at that point when he was at his darkest. Since Apius relinquished control of the book, Robert was able to continue on, and as you read, he became a valuable and trusted member of society."

Peter thought about that for a moment.

"Wouldn't it be a good thing for Apius to consume all of the evil?" Peter asked her. "Then you only have one evil person."

Miss Penntiworth smiled, remembering how great life was when it was as simple as only a child can make it.

"Unfortunately, it is not quite that easy Peter. Although Apius consumes the ink or absorbs the soul of the living, they are still out there. Empty shells of what they once were. Almost like puppets. Apius can command them to walk the earth and seek out people for him, or do evil acts that make others evil as well. They become a sort of army for Apius. None of us want to see that.

Once Apius has control of a person, there is no chance for them to redeem themselves from whatever evil they had done. Apius would never allow that, for that would weaken him."

They came to a part of the building Peter had never been before. The glass windows lining the room made it look like the Conservaory. Even the domed ceiling was made from glass, but this room was much smaller. Ornamental trees adorned the room, and the soft chirping of birds made everything feel new, like a warm spring day. Miss Penntiworth stopped, took a deep breath, smiled, and turned to Peter.

"Well, Peter, I must say, I have never had an arrival be as much of a handful as you have been," she told him, sounding almost sad.

"Is that good or bad?" he asked, his head hanging low to the ground.

Miss Penntiworth hesitated for a moment.

"Both, I believe," she said with a smile.

"What do you mean?" he asked her.

"Let's take a seat over here and enjoy the warmth of the room," she said as she led him to a nearby bench.

"I cannot comprehend being in this position for this long and expecting to know everything, or to be foolish enough to believe I have seen it all. I take something away from every experience I have, and you, Peter, have been quite an experience," she said as she smiled at him.

Peter noticed her eyes were glistening.

"I will certainly look back at this time and feel blessed for having met you," she told him.

"What's going on, Miss Penntiworth? What happens now?" he asked her.

"As I told you earlier, dear, today starts a new chapter in your life."

Peter still wasn't sure what she meant by that, and Miss Penntiworth didn't appear to want to let him know, but he felt he could still ask her some more questions. They might give him some clue as to what was going on.

"I can't see them letting me back into the Conservatory," he said.

"No, that cannot happen," Miss Penntiworth chuckled. "We have a different place for you."

There she goes again. he thought.

But the comment also caught him off guard. Why was everything so cryptic? Miss Penntiworth stood up and walked away, so Peter followed her.

"Will I enjoy this new place?" he asked, his voice quivering slightly.

"I cannot see why you would not, dear," she said.

What a safe answer. he thought.

Not comfortable with the uncertainty that was before him, Peter felt as though he was going to the doctor's office to get a shot. "That's never a good feeling," he muttered as he instinctively rubbed his arm for a moment.

Laying her hand on Peter's shoulder, Miss Penntiworth led him down an ornate hallway with arched stained-glass windows on both sides. He found himself lost in the beauty of the glass. Even the shadows it cast spilled brilliant colors across the white travertine floor. Each pane of glass depicted a different story in the artisan work in the glass. One showed a mother holding her newborn child to the sky as brilliant beams of sun burst from the clouds overhead. Another showed a family running through a meadow, holding on to a bright red kite which floated across the panes of glass.

Peter snapped back to his surroundings as Miss Penntiworth broke the silence.

"I just want you to know, Peter, that I will always remember you, and I will miss you greatly," she said.

Shocked, Peter looked up at her. He still wasn't certain where he was going, and even though he was scared at the thought of not seeing Miss Penntiworth any longer, he was feeling strangely calm and at ease. Nonetheless, Peter was at a loss for words.

"Will we get to visit each other?" he finally asked.

"I certainly hope it is written, dear, but rest assured, I will always be reading up on you, and I will know exactly what you are doing at every step of your life."

She gave him a warm smile and wrapped her arm around his shoulders as they continued to walk. Every time Peter saw Miss Penntiworth, she always seemed to be late for something, but today was different.

Why is she walking so slowly? he thought.

They came to an arched opening that was framed with white bricks. A wrought iron gate blocked them from going any further. Miss Penntiworth stood there and held onto one of the gate spindles. She then turned to Peter and smiled. From underneath her shawl, she pulled out a large metal ring with a dozen or so keys on it. She picked one out, inserted it into the lock, and unlocked the gate. It creaked loudly as she pulled the gate open.

Beyond the arched entry was a corridor that grew somewhat darker from where they stood. Peter tried to look down it, but the oil lamps lining the walls didn't provide enough light. They stood in silence for a moment. Miss Penntiworth didn't seem to be going anywhere, nor was Peter. He turned to her, unsure what to do next.

"I don't understand. What is this place?" he asked. "What am I supposed to do?"

"Unfortunately for us, Peter, we are not all-knowing. There is only One that knows all. We just have to have faith and believe we are in good hands."

Peter wasn't moving; he was too nervous for that. Miss Penntiworth turned to him.

"You need to believe, Peter," she told him. "There is nothing further I can tell you. You just have to have faith."

Peter swallowed hard and then started to walk through the gate. He hesitated for a moment as his whole body shook. There was too much uncertainty of what waited for him at the end of this corridor, and he didn't like it. He turned to Miss Penntiworth with his hand held out. She wouldn't, or couldn't, look at Peter, but she also held her hand out. Several minutes passed by, but neither Peter nor Miss Penntiworth would look at each other. He strained to hold back a tear as he thought about all the things they'd been through. After all of this time, she had become somewhat of a mother figure to him.

Still holding onto him, her hand warm and comforting, Miss Penntiworth finally got the courage to look at Peter. When she smiled and nodded to him, her eyes were filled with tears. He let go of Miss Penntiworth's hand and smiled back at her from the corner of his mouth. Taking a deep breath, Peter walked into the corridor and disappeared from her view. It had been too much of a struggle to keep from crying, so Peter made sure not to look back.

A short distance later, he came to a flight of stairs leading downward to the same darkness he'd been walking through. As he cautiously descended the stairs, it got brighter, and when he reached the bottom, he walked into a large room, better lit than the corridor he'd just left. Seven large floor candelabras were illuminated with a dozen lit candles in each. The walls were made from the same white bricks as before. Across the room was a solitary wooden door with a golden tapestry hanging over the top of it. The scene on the tapestry was similar to the ones in the stained-glass windows lining the hall. It showed a man and a woman holding a small baby wrapped in a blanket. Two cherubs flew above either side of the couple. On the left side of the door was a stone plaque embedded in the wall. Something was written on it, but there wasn't enough light in the room for Peter to see it clearly, so he took one of the candles from its holder, and walked over to the stone.

"When His lamp shone over my head, I walked through darkness," Peter read.

He wasn't sure what this writing meant, but after he read it, all of the nervousness, all of the aches and pains growing in his stomach, disappeared. He found himself more at ease. He tried the door, and when he opened it, he didn't hesitate as he walked into a surprisingly simplistic room. To this point, everything had been beautifully ornate, the Conservatory, the halls, the parks, but what Peter saw in this room was none of that.

Inside was nothing more than an ancient hand-carved wooden throne resting on top of a stone dais that was situated in the middle of the room. A golden light shined down from a circular opening in the ceiling, casting a brilliant light on the chair. The floor was nothing more than dirt, and there were no windows in the room.

Peter wasn't sure what he was supposed to do, so he stepped up onto the dais, turned to the chair, and slowly walked over to it. He looked for something that would explain what the chair was or what it symbolized. There were no plaques, directions, or even any carvings in the wood. There was nothing unusual about the chair other than the fact it looked extremely old. The wood was rough-hewn, and there were a series of small holes bored into the seat. Peter tried to move the chair, but it was embedded into the stone. Looking around the stone, he noticed a small metal spigot ingrained into the side of the dais. Peter hesitated for a moment before sitting in the chair. Even though he felt his heart racing, he wasn't afraid.

As Peter settled down onto the chair, he was immediately showered in the brilliant light shining down from the ceiling. Squinting, Peter looked up to see what the source of the light was. It seemed to be brighter than the sun, but it didn't hurt his eyes as he peered into it. Everything in the room vanished around him as he was enveloped in light and filled with warmth. It was a warmth he could feel streaming through his insides down to his toes. A calming feeling overcame Peter. He melted into the chair as he sat back. His mind, which had been racing with thoughts not thirty seconds ago, settled with him into the calm. He felt as though he was falling into a deep slumber, void of any stress or concerns. The more comfortable he felt in the chair, the more vivid the images around him became. He remembered Miss Penntiworth and how he'd felt every time she smiled at him. He smiled as he thought about the warm gooeyness of her chocolate chip cookies. He then recalled how good it felt to see there was a refuge for abused children, and how proud he was that it was named after him.

Emily then came into his thoughts. He smiled as he watched her dog, Jasper, sleeping quietly in her lap. Peter started to chuckle as he saw Mr. Grumsby in the bathtub with his rubber ducky and that goofy shower cap on his head. The images just kept coming, parading before him as he fondly looked back at his life. He thought about when he was alive, the day he made the baseball team and how he and his parents had eaten a whole cake that night in celebration. He'd been so happy, remembering how his father spun him around in celebration.

Peter's thoughts continued to flow out of him, and with each one, he felt happier and happier. The final thought he had was of his parents. Peter was staring up at them; his mother looked tired but happier than she'd ever been. His father was staring at Peter, too, and he heard him talking to his mother.

"Look at the three little freckles he has by his eye," his father said.

It was the only time Peter remembered seeing his father with a tear in his eye, but Peter knew it was because he was happy. Peter's hand reached out for them, and he saw it was small and chubby, just like a baby's hand, and with that, all became quiet, and darkness fell over the chair.

Several minutes later, Miss Penntiworth entered the room and smiled at the empty chair. She took a moment to reflect on a ten-year-old boy who came to her small but left a big impression in her heart. Walking over to the spigot, she removed a golden silk handkerchief from underneath her shawl and slowly, carefully, unwrapped it. Inside was a crystal ink jar, which she removed the cork from, setting it gently on the edge of the dais. Miss Penntiworth placed the ink jar underneath the spigot, and as she turned the handle, the golden liquid filled the jar. She closed the spigot, picked up the cork, and gingerly placed it into the jar. For the next several minutes, she sat there quietly, staring at the jar and smiling. She then stood and wrapped the crystal jar with the same golden handkerchief.

"Maybe next time, my dear Peter," she said as she turned her back to the room and shut the door.

CHAPTER 21
Goodbye?

As the evening sun dipped down into the distant ocean just outside of the Conservatory, an unknown assistant closed the book she had just finished reading. In the twilight shadows, she stood silently for a moment, looking at the name etched onto the front cover.

"Peter Nichols," she whispered as she slowly ran her hand over the lettering.

The book was thinner than most of the books whose pages she turned every day for the last however long. She continued to smile as she stared at the book.

"He sounded like a very nice boy," she said, wiping a tear from her eye.

As she carried the book down the ladder and over to a cart, she looked at the cover one more time before placing it into a purple sheath. The book was now no different than every other book that lay in her cart. She wheeled it out of the room and shut the two large wooden doors.

On the opposite end of the conservatory, Miss Penntiworth took another look at the precious ink jar. She smiled and slid the jar across the shelf, taking one last look before she closed and locked the door.

"We'll see each other again Peter."

The cold from the hallway shivered through her shoulders as she adjusted her shawl, just as a low, raspy laugh echoed in the distance.

Note from the Author

Word-of-mouth is crucial for any author to succeed. If you enjoyed the book, please leave a review online — anywhere you are able. Even if it's just a sentence or two. It would make all the difference and would be very much appreciated.

Thanks!
G.L.

About the Author

At the age of five, G. L. Garrett asked Santa for a typewriter. It was at that moment he knew he wanted to be an author. In the second grade, after mercilessly clacking away at the typewriter keys, he had his first story published in a local newspaper in Upstate New York. After a lengthy hiatus lasting several decades, G. L. Garrett took to writing again, giving way to a much quieter laptop.

Thank you so much for checking out one of our **Young Adult** novels.

If you enjoy our book, please check out our recommended title for your next great read!

Camp Strange by Renee Perez

"*Camp Strange*, in fact, is the best thing ever."

–KIRKUS REVIEWS

View other Black Rose Writing titles at
www.blackrosewriting.com/books and use promo code
PRINT to receive a **20% discount** when purchasing.

9 781684 333905